T0043863

THE
FIREBORNE
BLADE

ALSO BY CHARLOTTE BOND

The Watcher in the Woods

A Feast to Catch Souls

The Poisoned Crow

THE FIREBORNE BLADE

CHARLOTTE BOND

TOR PUBLISHING GROUP
NEW YORK

THE FIREBORNE BLADE

Copyright © 2024 by Charlotte Bond

Interior illustrations by Christine Foltzer

A Tordotcom Book
Published by Tom Doherty Associates / Tor Publishing Group
120 Broadway
New York, NY 10271

www.torpublishinggroup.com

Tor® is a registered trademark of Macmillan Publishing Group, LLC.

The Library of Congress Cataloging-in-Publication Data is available upon request.

ISBN 978-1-250-29031-1 (hardback)
ISBN 978-1-250-29032-8 (ebook)

Our books may be purchased in bulk for promotional, educational, or business use. Please contact your local bookseller or the Macmillan Corporate and Premium Sales Department at 1-800-221-7945, extension 5442, or by email at MacmillanSpecialMarkets@macmillan.com.

First Edition: 2024

Printed in the United States of America

0 9 8 7 6 5 4 3 2 1

To Nathan and Sophie *(meep)*

*For believing in me even
when I didn't believe in myself*

THE
FIREBORNE
BLADE

ONE

THE DEMISE AND DEMESNE OF DRAGONS
As told by Sir Nathaniel, Knight of the Grass

On my oath, I, Sir Nathaniel, do swear that what I am about to tell to the Distinguished Mage is the truth.

It was autumn in the year 651 since the Reckoning. It is not false modesty to say that I was one of the best three knights in the fourteen realms—maybe even as high as the second best. A dragon is a fearsome challenge, but also the dream of every knight. Being so skilled, I thought myself the perfect challenger for the Glebe-Reaver. I was so terribly, terribly wrong. I wish to tell my tale now so it is set down in history and may deter other knights from being as foolhardy as I was.

The Glebe-Reaver lived in a cave near the town of

Exenham, which lies in the Exen Valley. My squire—Tomas—and I ate heartily in an inn before we set out to confront the beast. I had a particularly good beef stew—I remember because it was as delicious going down as it was disgusting coming back up.

No one had seen the dragon in sixty years, although the grooves from its claws were visible in the surrounding fields. The farmers plant red clover in the furrows since the land is poisoned by those claws, and red clover is the only thing that grows there. I'm told it takes twenty seasons for the plant to soak up all the rot, making the land ready to till again.

I had done my research in the mage library, and I knew that the Glebe-Reaver generally slept for eighty to ninety years, so it should have been in the deepest part of its sleep cycle. I understand the dangers of killing a sleeping dragon, but still thought it better than the dangers of killing an awake one.

As with most dragon demesnes, there were no trees for about a quarter of a mile near to the cave entrance. We knew that the Glebe-Reaver's breath was toxic, and we had a special ointment to rub on the insides of our noses and mouths to decant the badness from the air. We had expected the stench to be a gradual thing that came upon us, but it was like running into a wall. One breath was easy and scented with the pleasant tang of autumn, the next burned my nose and throat. It made me feel as if someone held a noxious pillow over my face, smothering me in the foulest way possible. Tomas and I staggered back to the fresh air—that's when my stew made its return—and recovered ourselves before applying the salve that General Mage Thrax had given us. Please do pass on my thanks to him.

Once our noses and mouths were coated, we tried a second, more successful assault. The way to the dragon's lair was blessedly short, although we needed to reapply the salve before we reached the cavern, so insidious were those fumes.

It was a short battle. I had a sword General Mage Thrax had bespelled, and every strike I landed on the beast opened up a wound that kept growing. Because the Glebe-Reaver was asleep with its head elevated on a stone ledge, I was unable to deal it an instant, killing blow to its brain like Sir Gaius—although, given his end, perhaps matters were in my favour. It was a thrust to the chest that ultimately did it for the beast, not because it hit a vital organ but because the wound opened so wide that its guts flopped out of its internal cavity and landed on the sandy ground.

I have been on the battlefield, and I have seen men try to stuff their insides back into their bodies. That is exactly what the dragon did, letting out pitiable keening noises as it did so.

I have hunted with kings and knights, and I have never seen a beast do such a thing. I mention this now because it led me to wonder just what kind of mind resides in a dragon's scaly skull, whether it is as bestial as we assume. However, I am but a humble knight, and I know the honoured mages will be able to make a better study of such a thing than I.

Having read the earlier volumes of *The Demise and Demesne*

of Dragons as well as having listened to other knights speak of their experiences, I know it's possible to tell the instant a dragon dies because of how the magic in the air changes. So it was with the Glebe-Reaver. My ears popped, my mouth filled with bile, and a blasting hot wind scathed my skin for several heartbeats.

Once we knew the dragon was truly dead, we waited a few moments to see what would happen. You can't kill a magical beast without consequences. When nothing dreadful happened immediately, we began gathering up the coins, gems, and more valuable items in its lair. You know how it is—those beasts will seize anything of metal, but not all metal is valuable. There was an anvil, several copper bathtubs, a gilded hairbrush—all sorts of trivial and worthless items.

It was Tomas who first noticed the sludge, and I will be forever in his debt. I myself was examining a set of cutlery when Tomas cried out, "Master! Behind you! Stand still!"

The creature's guts had started to turn into a black bubbling sludge that inched its way across the cave floor. A thin line of it had already spread between me and the exit. In retrospect, I should have jumped then, immediately. But I wanted to secure some of the treasure. You probably know this—most of the realm does—but my father has debts, and I wanted to bring something home. So I knotted my sack of treasure and tossed it over to Tomas. He darted forward to snatch it up before returning to a place of safety, but we both saw what that bubbling black mass did: it oozed towards him like it had a mind of its own. All this could only have taken twenty seconds, no more, but in that time, the pool of ichor separating me from the exit had grown. I knew I had to act straightaway or risk it becoming too large to jump. I was on a large stone, the better to reach a stash of treasure in a crevice, so I could not take a run-up. Instead, I leaned back against the wall and pushed myself off. I cleared the sludge, I really did, and I remember a moment of pure elation before that horrible substance surged over my foot.

When I was a squire, I got drunk with some friends and ended up walking through a campfire. Given my flimsy shoes, I was lucky to escape severe burns, but I remember the heat and the pain.

This heat was worse, the pain tripled.

I staggered forward and away from the foul stuff, my plate armour dripping off my feet like silver treacle; my flesh followed soon after.

As I stumbled away, I glanced fearfully over my shoulder and saw the sludge surging after me. It was as if a taste of my flesh had invigorated it. Before, it had moved sluggishly, but there was no mistaking its hungry, malevolent motion now.

My right foot was now nothing more than a stub of bone, and I was unbalanced enough that I nearly toppled to the ground. It was Tomas who saved me. He caught me and acted as a crutch all the way to the cave entrance. I can't tell you the bliss I felt to lurch out into the sunlight—I had thought never to see it again.

When we were a safe distance from the entrance, Tomas lowered me to the ground and saved my life for a second time by cutting away the poisoned flesh of my leg with his knife. I'm convinced that if he had not, that poisonous ichor would have spread through my veins. I believe I passed out due to pain, but afterwards, he showed me the blackened patches of earth where my flesh had befouled the ground. The blade of his knife was smoking, and over the course of a day, it shriveled away into nothing.

I owe that young man my life. The people of Exenham owed us their livelihoods because we rid them of a pestilential beast that had blighted their fields for almost two centuries. It was a task that needed completing, but there was no glory or thrill in it.

And that's all I have to say on the matter.

Note by General Mage Thrax: The Glebe-Reaver was aged circa 365 years and had been in its demesne near Exenham nearly all its life. Distinguished Mage Mair and Lower Mages Rushmere and Olton visited the area six months after the dragon's death. They took scrapings of the sludge using a diamond chisel, the instrument necessary as the substance had hardened considerably. Apparently, the locals had had some success in retrieving larger items from the sludge for up to a week after the Glebe-Reaver's death before the substance hardened to the point of securing everything in place. Since those items recovered in this manner were partly dissolved, they were only of use as scrap metal.

During their operations, one villager accidentally stumbled and put a hand out to steady himself, plunging it right into a patch of sludge. By all accounts, the local physick tried to save him, but the man wouldn't sit still and was too hysterical to take quieting syrup. The physick was unable to remove all the tainted flesh, resulting in the ichor traveling through the man's veins and into his heart in just two days.

The patches on the grass where Nathaniel's flesh fell were still black and barren when most recently investigated.

Samples of the dragon's death matter are held in the library archives marked with 651/GR/N/1–9.

TWO

Maddileh swayed slightly and glanced over her shoulder. Just a few steps away was the outside world filled with early-summer sunshine, the air stirred by playful zephyrs, the birds singing their joy at the world reborn. Inside the gloomy tunnel, it felt as if she'd crossed from one glorious world into a dank and dangerous one. For a terrible moment, she thought about throwing down her weapons and walking back out into the world behind her. For innumerable nights, her dreams had been filled with fire. Dragon hunting was a fool's game, and she should never have come, the king's command be damned.

But what choice did she have? Leering, mocking faces rose up in her mind. The snide whispers, the sly glances as she walked the tourney fields, trying to be equal among men who saw her as nothing but a cast-off woman, all because she'd been stupid enough to fall in love with a cruel man.

Who could love a thing like you? What kind of thing are you anyway? Neither knight nor lady. She winced as Sir Allerbon's words echoed in her head. She'd given him a lock of her hair, her trust, and her heart, and he had taken them and crushed them. Now she knew she should have just walked away, should have resisted the urge to punch his smug, grinning face, but retrospection was pointless now that she'd been banished. Besides, broken hearts did not listen to reason, and if she lived that moment again, she'd probably still punch him.

No. There was no place on the tourney field for her now; the king had confiscated her armour. She needed the Fire-borne Blade if she was to regain her standing. She had to go on. Reflexively, her fingers went to curl around the spear, only to find that her hand was empty. She spun round, her eyes scanning the floor. Where was it? How could she have dropped it? *When* had she dropped it? She'd only just entered the tunnel a few minutes before.

"Looking for this, mistress?" The voice startled her, as she'd thought herself alone in the tunnel. Emerging from a little way down was a tall, lanky young man who looked younger than Maddileh in all respects except his gaze, which was flinty, cold, and assessing. He was holding out a spear—it must be hers, but the markings on it looked different. No. Wait. It was the spear she'd taken from the Weldrake Repository. She remembered now. Staring at the enchanted engravings made her head ache.

The young man stretched his arm out a little farther. "This is your spear, mistress," he said, but there was the slightest tinge of anxiety in his voice.

Maddileh's squires were with her for so little time that she barely remembered their names. This one had escaped her completely. "*Master*," she said curtly. "Not *mistress*. Mistresses run houses or warm beds. A squire calls his knight *master,* and that's what you will call me."

A slight curl of his lip indicated his distaste.

So, he's going to be one of those squires.

"Sorry, Master, I meant no offence." The young man's manner, tone, and posture were that of a perfect servant now, his distaste completely hidden. It was never good to have a squire who could lie so convincingly.

"If you were a half-decent squire, you should know that a knight never carries her own weapons unless there is immediate danger."

His answering smile was obsequious. "But surely when one is walking through the demesne of a dragon, danger is always imminent, so—"

Maddileh stepped forward and was gratified to see the squire step back, his eyes wide with alarm. A tall woman, she could easily meet his gaze on a level.

"What is your name, boy?" she demanded. She saw the flash of anger in his eyes; very few squires liked to be referred to as *boy* by a woman, especially not one who almost looked of an age with her. She'd had squires before who'd resented seeking employment with her, driven by desperation rather than choice; they could be so sullen and disobedient that not only could she not teach them anything, sometimes she couldn't even save them. It was important, with such squires, to establish the hierarchy early.

"Petros," he said finally, courteously.

"Well, Petros, would you care to explain to me why you are here?"

He suddenly looked hunted. "You hired me, Master. To be your squire."

Maddileh had a vague recollection of meeting this man, thinking him too old and opinionated to be her squire; there must have been something about him that had convinced her to take him on. But her head was hurting, and everything seemed muddled. That had to be the dragon magic taking effect; sometimes it crept up on you; sometimes it hit you all at once.

"I know what I'm getting out of this arrangement," Maddileh persisted, although she suspected that what she'd be getting was a whole lot of trouble, "but what are you getting? What do you hope to learn or achieve while you're in my service?"

She watched his expression as various answers evidently went through his mind. "I want to be there when you get the Fireborne Blade, Master. I want to share in your glory and be a part of the tales." There was honesty to his answer, but a sullenness too. She sensed he was hiding something; she wondered what it was and whether it would be the death of him.

Or her.

Suddenly, the world lurched to the side, and she leaned against the wall, trying not to be sick.

"That'll be the magic, Master," Petros said. "Pockets of it drift out like little bubbles of confusion or fear. You walk through one and then you forget why you're there and turn around to go home, or you become so afraid you run away.

It muddles you or makes you sick. It does anything it can to make you leave."

With her stomach a bit easier, Maddileh straightened and studied him thoughtfully. "You know your stuff about dragons, then?"

"Oh yes, Master. I have read all four volumes of *Demise and Demesne*."

"Really? All four?"

"It took quite a while."

"Then perhaps you'll be useful to me after all."

He bowed. "I do hope so, Master. Shall we start if you're recovered?"

"Have you a light?"

"Yes, indeed." He reached inside one of the satchels over his shoulder. With great care, he pulled out what looked like a crystal ball. Bringing it close to his lips, he whispered some unheard words; a speck of light came to life in the orb's centre, growing in size and intensity until the tunnel was brightly illuminated.

"Magic," said Maddileh with distaste.

Petros looked at her with surprise. "You don't like magic? But the spear, your armour—"

"I use it when I must, but I don't have to like it."

"I see." He gave her a look that was bordering on contempt, and then he was all solicitude again. "I am pleased to tell you that this orb will not only provide us with light, it should also guide us down the right path."

It's an orb of direction as well as of light, then, Maddileh thought. *Where did a squire get money to buy that? Because it's certainly not mine. Or is it?*

Although Maddileh couldn't deny the usefulness of a single object that provided both light and direction, she'd much rather use burning torches than light orbs. Less chance of the magic escaping and doing something terrible to you. But even she had to admit that the mage orbs not only provided better light but also avoided the need to carry fuel rags and matches in their supplies.

Not willing to be fully won over, she said, "I have a map for directions."

"Perhaps we could examine them both when choosing our path, Master?" It was a reasonable suggestion, and in the maze of a dragon's demesne, every advantage should be utilised. If she refused the assistance of magic, it would be through stubbornness and irritation rather than logic.

"Both of them, then," she conceded. "Let's start down this tunnel. The sooner we reach the White Lady's lair, the sooner we can return to light and the outside world." It had to be her imagination, but Maddileh felt sure she detected a rumble in the earth as if a great beast somewhere had growled, its ears pricking at the sound of its name.

If Petros noticed, he didn't say anything but merely started down the passageway. Before she followed him, Maddileh glanced over her shoulder at the sunlit world where blossoms danced like snowflakes on the breeze. She'd descended into dragon lairs before—twice, in fact—and neither time had she felt with such certainty that she would never see the outside world again. She stared at the spiraling blooms; something felt wrong about them, but she couldn't say what.

Curse this blasted dragon magic!

"Master?" Petros called out from ahead.

"Coming." Maddileh turned from the sunlight and walked into whatever the darkness held for her.

THREE

THE DEMISE AND DEMESNE OF DRAGONS

The Passing of the Beldam, 643 years from the Reckoning
As told by Sir Warbrick, Knight of the Blue Sands, to General Mage
Thrax

On my oath, I, Sir Warbrick, do swear that what I am about to tell to the General Mage and Distinguished Mages here assembled is the truth.

They may call her the hag of dragons, but that old creature was tough, I can tell you.

You don't get to be as old as the Beldam without being a mean old bitch. And female dragons are far more vicious than males—did you know that?

[GM Thrax: Sir Warbrick, if we could keep to your

personal experiences rather than straying into well-known facts, I would count it as a favour.]

Of course, of course—all you men in that shiny fortress of yours know all there is to know about dragons from your orbs and your books and your whispers.

[GM Thrax: If we could—]

Yes, fine. Don't rush me.

The demesne was easy to find. I paid some villagers to take me right to the cave mouth. I'd brought with me an orb of direction, but we didn't really need it. The tunnel went straight down into the Beldam's lair. She was prowling around down there, guarding her treasure, grumbling, but even so, I still managed to take her by surprise.

[GM Thrax: Our records show that she'd already been—]

If you're going to repeat Dolomere's claim that he injured her and I had it easy, then that's complete rot.

[GM Thrax: What I was *going* to say was that I imagined an injured dragon would be twice as unpleasant and on her guard.]

Precisely! That's what she was—prowling and on her guard. But luckily, we had various enchanted weapons with us. I tell you, that tough old girl had me down to the last one. My other spell-forged weapons hardly made a dent, but the ash spear finally did for her. I got it through a gap in her scales, and it must have pierced her heart I thrust it in so far.

Have you ever heard a dragon's dying scream? Not through one of those seeing orbs—I mean up close. It's deafening. Terrifying. You have to be a brave man to withstand it.

Well, once I'd struck her heart, it was like . . . saying

darkness fell isn't quite right. It was more as if a wave of darkness rolled out from her corpse, washing through the cave and over me. For a second, I just stood there because . . . well, because it was unnerving, very much so. At first, there was this awful, heavy silence, such as when your ears fill with water. Then I started hearing noises. Voices, sort of, but also not. I imagined, at the time, in the dark, that they were the voices of the people she'd killed. Oh, I know they *say* dragons don't kill people—only if they're rabid or extremely hungry—

[GM Thrax: Or if they're knights come to kill them.]

But these voices, their words, their pleas . . .

[GM Thrax: Were they like the dragon-dead you meet in the tunnels?]

You mean the ghosts? Never met one. I don't think they exist. I think Dolomere just claims one touched him because only a coward suffers from screaming nightmares. Better to say it's the touch of a ghost, ha!

[GM Thrax: And, of course, the Beldam was the first dragon you'd ever pursued.]

It takes only one dragon to make a knight's name, and the Beldam was more than enough for me. Anyway, it went all dark, there were some terrifying voices, and I ran. Like I said, there was but a single tunnel down into the lair. I dare say I would have been a dead man if there had been more.

[GM Thrax: I see. And your squire—Eglin, I believe he was called—what happened to him?]

That miserable little wretch left me at the cave entrance before we'd gone twenty steps. I had to carry my own damn weapons. He ran home to his piss-drunk father, I've no doubt, although I suspect he was eaten by wolves before he got there.

[GM Thrax: But you said *we* didn't really need the orb of direction. *We.*]

Yes, but that's just—

[GM Thrax: You also said: "Luckily, *we* had various enchanted weapons with *us.*" See, Sir Warbrick, it's written down.]

You're twisting my words. Eglin ran off, I tell you. Go ask his father. That cowardly wretch must be home by now.

[GM Thrax: We have already spoken to Mr. Tilney. We asked him to identify a voice on one of our speaking orbs.]

A voice?

[GM Thrax: Yes. We sent two Lower Mages to record some of the voices that you reported. Most of them had faded by the time they'd got there. Of course, I don't need to tell a famous knight like you that the explosion of magic that follows a dragon's demise will fade over time. This can be anywhere from a few hours to a few decades. It seems that the voices hanging on the longest were those the dragon had killed most recently. The second-to-last one we've identified as a farmer Belter, who died seven decades ago protecting his pigs. But the last one was a more recent death. Much more recent. Would you like to hear it?]

I would not. I've listened to enough ridiculous talk about ghosts.

[GM Thrax: Nevertheless—Lower Mage Hutton, set alight the speaking orb so that the Knight of the Blue Sands can hear the testimony of the speaker.]

{LM Hutton fetches and activates the orb, which speaks thusly}

Oh, thank the gods, there's someone here. Can you hear me? {Inaudible reply} Oh, thank you. I thought I was lost. Can you lead me out? {Inaudible reply} Oh, it was the most dreadful thing—it was the Beldam. My master struck her with a spear good and proper, and then this darkness . . . this darkness whooshed over us, and it was so silent, but then there were all these voices. I was stunned and frightened at first, but then my master—the Knight of the Blue Sands, you know—he was crying out in terrible fear. Something was trying to drag him away, I think. So I rushed forward, following his voice. I had my knife ready—just a dagger, but it's enchanted to carve up ghosts, you see. So I thought: *If the ghosts have gotten him, I can free him.* And I found him and slashed all around him. The blade doesn't cut flesh or metal—only insubstantial creatures—and freed him. We stumbled towards the entrance and were hurrying up the tunnel when the ghosts caught up with us again. I freed myself first, then I could hear from my master's screams that they were dragging him back into the cave. So I went back for him and cut him free a second time. He was sobbing and shrieking, "Not me! Not me!" And I thought that maybe they'd driven him mad. I know dragon ghosts can haunt you with a touch, plague you with bad dreams of their deaths or worse, so I thought maybe we'd been touched too. Only . . . I can't really explain . . . I felt a nudge—well, more like a shove really—as my master got up. He had his hands on my arms, but in his panic, he pushed me backward. Maybe he thought I was a ghost made real or something. Anyway, then the ghosts were on me. I dropped my knife, and their hands were everywhere. I called out so that my master could find me in the darkness, but there was no response. I managed to escape by . . . by . . . well, I can't really remember, but I did, and now I'm so worried they have him too. I'm sure I heard him running ahead of me, but those ghosts were so fast. He must be here somewhere. Can you help me look for him in this terrible darkness? I have to look for him. I can't leave him here. Will you help me find him? Please, I can't take much more of this terrible place.

{LM Hutton deactivates the orb}

[GM Thrax: There was quite a bit more, but that is the most elucidating bit. Is there anything you would like to add to your statement, Sir Warbrick?]

{ten beats of silence}

No.

[GM Thrax: Then this interview is at an end. Thank you for your words, Sir Warbrick. They will help posterity. Please exit through the door behind you. I believe there is someone in the corridor who wishes to speak with you.]

FOUR

Maddileh was on fire. She was surrounded by flames. They were on her skin and under it. Her teeth throbbed, her eyes were white agony.

She sat bolt upright, breathing heavily, the panic of the nightmare still clawing at her chest. The air was cold and damp, but she relished each clammy breath.

"Ghost dreams?" Petros asked. He was boiling up some thyme tea over a little portable stove.

"No," said Maddileh more sharply than she'd intended. "Just a nightmare." She swallowed, her throat raw as if she'd been screaming. "Is that tea ready?"

"Yes, Master. Here." Petros handed her a tin cup with sweet, spicy steam rising from it. She noticed a familiar item on his wrist: a bracelet made of a bloodred ribbon interwoven with hair. She grinned and pulled back the sleeve of her own tunic to show five similar bracelets. "I see we are of the same mind. But you should know that each braid will only repel one ghost."

"Perhaps yours might, Master, but my shade bracelet was created by the High Mage himself, with the hair of a dying princess. It will last me more than one ghost."

"High Mage Hosh himself?" Maddileh mused as she

sipped the tea. "I thought he was half-dead. What is he doing making a shade charm for a nobody squire?"

Petros's face stiffened as if he was trying to hide his true expression. "He is not well, it's true, but I believe he made this quite some time ago. And I have it because I am *not* a nobody squire—my family are actually quite influential."

"And your family are . . . ?"

She didn't think he would tell her, but then he said, "The Silverlocks." She was impressed, but suspicious too. The Silverlocks were one of the wealthiest families in the fourteen realms. Their sons were knights, politicians, mages—never squires.

"I can see why the High Mage granted your request, then."

"Would you care for some squirrel?" Petros asked, pulling strips of jerky out of one of his satchels.

"No. Thank you."

He shrugged and put it away.

After a moment's silence, she said as kindly as she could, "Your bracelet might have been woven by the High Mage himself, but in my experience, even the most powerful charms only work once against ghosts."

"Oh yes?" It was clear from his tone that she'd pricked his pride. "And I suppose you've seen dozens of braids woven by a High Mage."

"No," she said, allowing him a moment of smugness before she added, "only one. I accompanied the Knight of the Woven Stars when he was sent by his father to try to reclaim the gold from the lair of the Silken Sigh. The dragon had been dead some eighty years by that point, but the demesne was still haunted by all those villagers who had died during her death throes. Sir Alfonso's father had begged the Mage Guild for something to protect his fourth son from the dragon-dead."

Petros snorted. "Fourth son? I'm surprised his father cared at all."

Maddileh studied him, then asked, "What number son are you?"

Petros swiftly dropped his gaze. After an awkward moment, he said, "So, what happened to the Knight of the Woven Stars? I don't think I read about him."

"He survived the trip, but we didn't get very far. We were about a quarter of the way across the Barrens and had met around a dozen ghosts before one noticed us and got close enough to touch my master. The braid flared a bright, blinding white; the shade stumbled back and then vanished. The High Mage had promised Sir Alfonso that the braid would keep him safe from all and any dragon-dead, but it burned away after just one, like they all do. I guess even the High Mage can't cheat death magic, although I understand he's doing pretty well at keeping his own demise at bay. How old is he now? Around a hundred and fifty, isn't it?"

"Almost two hundred," Petros said distractedly. He was anxiously twisting the shade bracelet around his wrist, a frown on his face. "But he's still as sharp as a mage in the prime of life—so I've heard anyway. So if he says this braid will protect against more than one ghost, then surely . . ." His voice trailed off.

Maddileh looked down at her own collection of charm bracelets. Now that she looked closely, she saw that one of the braids was lacking a ribbon. She fingered it thoughtfully. Shade bracelets were items she bought whenever she could. Most of the time, they were in good supply, but sometimes—like the last few months—they might be in demand and hard to get hold of. This usually coincided with a dragon waking, when a host of squires and knights decided to turn their hands to dragon hunting. There were two schools of thought as to when to hunt a dragon. Villagers were more likely to complain about an awake dragon and would declare the knight who rid them of it a hero. But an alert dragon is suspicious and cunning, a deadly foe. Killing a sleeping dragon was easier, but the way into their lair was more perilous as a dragon's dreams could take form and stalk the tunnels. But in either case, the dragon-dead were an ever-present danger, and shade bracelets were the surest defence against them.

Of course, the White Lady had been awake for over eighty years, or so they said. No catching her off her guard.

Maddileh considered her bracelets again. She could remember where she'd gotten three of them, but was uncertain where the other two, including the one lacking a ribbon, had come from. Did it serve a different purpose if it had no ribbon? She couldn't remember, and her ignorance gnawed at her. What else had this cursed dragon magic forced her to forget?

Draining her tea, she handed the cup back to Petros, who packed it away while she got out the map. Petros moved closer to look at it too. Maddileh had traced their path so far with a piece of charcoal; the Mage Guild paid handsomely for accurate lair maps. Some of the tunnels on the parchment ended with a dotted line, indicating what lay beyond was unknown.

"How many people died here to get this much of a map, do you think?" Petros asked softly.

"I don't know, but I guess many. The White Lady is old. These tunnels have been here longer than the High Mage. Generally, she doesn't venture abroad much more, and they say she only sleeps lightly, if at all."

"They say she can speak too," said Petros.

"I doubt that. My father had a Distinguished Mage to dinner one night and he spent quite some time explaining how the tongue and facial muscles of a dragon can't form words—or, at least, human words. Maybe she speaks dragon, some language we can't understand, but if so, why haven't other people heard other dragons speaking it? The books would mention it.

"Now, come on. Let's get going. Get the orb to start moving again, will you?"

FIVE

SIX MONTHS AGO

If she could avoid it, Maddileh never worked for mages. She didn't trust them. There were more bad tales about them than good ones. The righteous helped heal blighted villages, found where crucial missing documents might be stored in their great library, and could light a peasant's fire of wet twigs with a snap of their fingers, ensuring that the fire blazed all night—maybe even all winter. But the bad ones pried out secrets to blackmail rich nobles, sent shadow hags against you if you slighted them, or could make a potion that would turn you as solid as stone until they deemed you had learned your lesson.

Magic was banned in tournaments, so while she had been competing, she'd been able to distance herself from the whole distasteful business. But recent incidents had not just left a black mark on her tourney sheet but torn it up completely. While Maddileh wanted to blame Sir Allerbon for all her trouble, she knew she was as much to blame as he. She should have kept her temper. She should have ignored the gibes. She should not have fallen in love with him in the first place, and she certainly shouldn't have believed his lie that he loved her.

Who could love a thing like you? What kind of thing are you anyway? Neither knight nor lady.

Maddileh regretted everything, from going willingly to his bed and giving him a lock of her hair to punching the smug grin off his face and holding a knife to his throat within sight of the king. It was only King Cyron's special regard for her that had kept him from stripping her of all her titles. And it was only by obeying his last words to her— "Prove your worth to me, Sir Maddileh, in some way that will justify my faith in you"—that she would regain her armour and be counted as honourable.

And how do you justify the faith of a king? Much less one known as "the Blessed and Noble." The Fireborne Blade, that's how. Retrieving the weapon and presenting it to King Cyron was the only way to rid herself of her past offences.

Everyone knew the legendary blade was held by the White Lady, and numerous knights had died trying to recover it. The odds were not in her favour, but with her disgrace weighing heavily on her, Maddileh would prefer a swift and fiery death to the half life she was forced to live now.

Better death than this life, she thought as she stood outside the meeting hall of the Harbeck chapter of the Mage Guild. The town was so small it barely showed up on a map, but she'd heard whispers on the tourney circuit that the mage in these parts, Distinguished Mage Kennion, had information that could help her against the White Lady. Still, a mage was a mage, and Maddileh was close to having second thoughts as she stood outside the somewhat-aged building with its peeling paint. But as she shifted uneasily, there was the faint crackle of paper from the inside pocket of her jerkin. It was a letter from her mother. Despite Maddileh burying herself in the far-flung reaches of the Eighth Realm, the letter had found her.

This recent disgrace with the Knight of the Golden Tree shows that it's time to give up on your ridiculous ambitions and come home. Please come back and be my beloved daughter.

Just thinking of those words made her stomach curdle, as if the eels in the pie she'd eaten earlier had come alive and were writhing in her gut.

"I cannot go back. I *will not* go back," she said, clutching the hilt of her sword. That sword—gifted to her on her eighteenth birthday by King Cyron himself—had nearly been taken from her by an angry mob that had ambushed her the night of her disgrace. It had been a hard and horrible fight, but she'd kept her sword and sent her attackers limping away.

"If this sword ever leaves my hand," she'd shouted after them, "it will be because *I* chose it and *I* lay it down."

Now, standing in the drizzle before the Mages' Hall, she said softly, "No time to lie down and rest just now, old friend. We have work to do."

And if I'm to get the Fireborne Blade, I'm going to need some help. Gritting her teeth, she went up to the door and knocked.

Distinguished Mage Kennion was a tall, bony man with ink-stained fingers. He had a warm smile and a pleasant, attentive expression that made you feel as if every word you spoke had value. However, his eyes were guarded and alert, flicking over her face as he watched for every twitch, every tell, and every thought.

"Welcome, Sir Maddileh," he said, leading her through into the hall, which was set up with a selection of circular tables, each with five chairs around them. While there were clay cups and jugs of wine on every table, there were also inkwells, pens, and parchment. "We each have different things to discuss," Kennion said as he took her around the hall, "and debates can get quite heated, so some decent space between us all is required. We have put wards on all the windows and the main door, but we always keep the back door free of any charms. There was . . . an incident where a chapter's charms were corrupted against them. Rather than stopping people coming in, the words stopped those inside from getting out. A few burning torches through the window and . . ." He spread his hands in a gesture of "you can guess the rest."

"Nasty way to die," Maddileh said sincerely.

"Indeed. Like being incinerated by a dragon, I imagine," Kennion said, watching her carefully.

"I've heard that dragon breath is a far less painful death. Their flames burn so hot it's over in an instant. Trapped in a burning building, you've got smoke to choke you, flames to eat you slowly. I'd sooner death by dragon, thank you."

"I believe you have the right of it," Kennion mused, adjusting a corn dolly that hung on the wall; Maddileh saw an insectile leg reach between gaps in the weaving and try to stab Kennion's fingers. He paid it no mind. "Dragon fire is such a quick death that I've seen orbs where the ghosts of deceased knights and squires didn't even know they were dead, poor devils."

"Do you think you'll be actively attacked tonight?" Maddileh asked, wanting to turn the conversation away from such unsettling topics.

"If I didn't, do you think I would have incurred the expense of a knight to guard us?"

She'd heard that the mages were split into three factions. One set strongly supported the High Mage, believing that his wisdom would continue the wealth and prosperity the fourteen realms were currently enjoying and that his quest to extend his life even further than his current longevity was justified by the wisdom he could bestow on the realms. Another sect believed that he had lived long enough and that his ideas were as old as he was; they sought to displace him, although no one would be brave or stupid enough to try to assassinate him. They just wanted time to take its course. A third faction was vacillating between the two, swapped sides depending on which section was prevalent on any particular day.

"I find it best not to second-guess the thoughts of a mage, sir," Maddileh replied carefully. "Your minds are often occupied by things that we commoners can't comprehend." She cursed herself for her sarcasm; she needed this job, and now her smart mouth might have jeopardised that.

Kennion raised an eyebrow. "The Knight of the Stairs can hardly call herself a commoner. Tales of your famous deeds and actions have reached even our backwater. The famous stand by which you earned your name. The patronage of the king—even though females are rarely allowed into the ranks of noble knights."

"And no doubt you've heard of my disgrace as well," Maddileh said, sensing where this was going and wanting to preempt the final blow. Kennion stared at her thoughtfully for a few heartbeats.

"I know how it can be for women in a man's world. My own great-grandmother was one of the very few female Sub-Grand Mages in the history of the Guild—did you know that?"

"I did. Sub-Grand Irma, if I recall."

Kennion laughed delightedly. "Indeed! Well recalled. I remember her story particularly because she would not be known by her last name. She made the others call her Irma, enjoying the discomfort of those forced to say a female name. But you're frowning, knight."

"I am. I'd read that she went by her first name because the other mages refused to acknowledge her as a part of the Guild. They wanted her to feel forever set apart and unworthy."

"Ah, we are all puppets of history. What people remember about us is what is written down, and who has the power to influence writers after their own deaths? Doesn't it make you wonder what will be written about us by those who come after?"

"I try not to dwell on such things, sir. And for what it's worth, I thought your great-grandmother was an inspiration, whatever her name."

"I thought she might appeal to you—a woman who chose not to shorten her name to 'Madds,' a neutral name that would not have drawn comments on the tourney lists, especially when a helmet covered your face."

Silence held between them for a few moments, and Maddileh realised that she was growing to like Kennion, just a little bit.

"Have you seen all you need, sir knight?" he asked her.

"Yes, thank you, Distinguished One. But may I ask one more question? Do you have any idea of who might attack you?"

"Oh, any and all, I should imagine," he said, his eyes drifting to a platter of savoury tarts that a serving girl had recently brought in.

"But do you have any specific individuals I should be on the lookout for? I can defend this place better if I know the particulars of any threat you face."

Kennion withdrew his hand from the tarts, a thoughtful expression on his face. He glanced around the room, then said, "I wouldn't say this to just any common thug, but a knight—especially the Knight of the Stairs—would have the wisdom and tact to keep what I am about to say to herself. There are divisions, shall we say, within the Guild. We all of us revere and respect the High Mage, of course, but some of us feel that his constant search for longevity is distracting to him. There are dark powers massing beyond our borders, and a High Mage should be turning his mind to such matters rather than dwelling on impossible cures that will extend his years further."

"I see." Maddileh kept her face carefully blank. His confidence in her was flattering.

But then, she reflected, *I am a disgraced knight—for all his fine words of trusting my discretion, who would believe me if I repeated such rumours?*

"Do you think an attack is likely or just possible?" she asked.

Before he could answer, the door behind them opened with such force that it thudded against the wall. Maddileh spun round, drawing her short sword in a swift movement and pointing it at the throat of the intruder, who turned out to be the serving girl from before, a fruit basket in her arms. She was shorter than Maddileh, but that wasn't saying much since most women were shorter and slimmer than the Knight of the Stairs. The woman's brown hair curled under her chin, framing her oval face and a pair of smoky-grey eyes that had widened when faced with a drawn blade. However, the woman's instant of shock was quickly replaced by one of disdain. "Don't point that thing at me, you idiot. I'm supposed to be here."

Maddileh glanced at Kennion before she lowered the weapon. The mage, stepping forward and slightly between the women, explained, "This is Saralene, my maid, my clerk, my confidante, my right hand."

Your lover too? Maddileh thought, taking care that such suspicions did not show on her face.

"You see this amulet?" Kennion said, indicating a pendant around Saralene's neck. "That is sister to the wards I made for the building. Only mages may pass through the protections I've put on the doors, but this will allow Sara-lene to pass in and out without setting off any alarms."

"Do I need one too? I'm not a mage either," Maddileh asked.

"Strangely, no. The wards seem not to work on those who've uttered the knightly oath to the king. It must be something in the manner of the words required."

"Couldn't you just amend the wards to keep out knights as well? That'd be safest."

"It's not that simple," Saralene said, a hint of haughtiness to her voice. "Words are powerful, and tweaking spells is not advised." Her voice had the tone of a lesson learned by rote.

"Besides," said Kennion, beaming at them both, "why do I need to worry about knights attacking when I have my very own champion on hand?"

"Have you warned her about Old Jamie, sir?" Saralene asked as she put down the fruit on a sideboard.

"Oh! Thank you for reminding me. Yes, Sir Maddileh, I should mention that there's a rather ancient drunk who wanders the town on fine evenings, looking for dwellings or taverns where he might inveigle himself and perhaps secure a bellyful of ale. He sauntered in here once, and the poor fellow nearly got decapitated by a secondary ward. Feeling bad for the man, who was very shaken, I sat him down and let him eat his fill before sending him on his way. I must say, there were some of us who found his garrulous tales quite the diversion.

"Anyhow, my kindness was an error since he clearly de-cided that free food and ale was associated with this place and has tried to come back during subsequent meetings. Near decapitation did not appear to be much of a deterrent, and it seemed that by outwitting my wards once, he was able to do so again, which was both peculiar and worrying. I tried putting charms of confusion around the entrance, but Old Jamie is so drunk already that a little extra confusion doesn't seem to distract him. He's wandered into *four* secret meetings. Four! I'm reasonably confident that even a Sub-Grand Mage could not gain entry past my charms, and yet they do not keep Old Jamie out."

"And you have no idea why he can get past your wards while no one else can? Doesn't that worry you? Shouldn't you be trying to find out why?"

Saralene spun round and snapped, "You shouldn't question the Distinguished One in such a rude—"

"Saralene, it is quite all right," Kennion said soothingly.

"It's not as if we don't have bigger problems to look into," the servant muttered.

"Saralene." Kennion's voice was sharp and dangerous. "That is enough."

Saralene turned away from them, her cheeks red.

"What shall I do if I encounter him?" Maddileh asked.

Saralene walked over and thrust at her a battered flask along with a bundle of what turned out to be bread, cheese, and cold bacon wrapped up. "Give him these and send him on his way."

"That's very kind of you," Maddileh said to Kennion.

"Oh, it's not my idea. The old drunkard has Saralene to thank for that. My solution was going to be to add in another decapitation spell." He winked before wandering off to check on last-minute arrangements.

Maddileh's eyes went to Saralene's face. Her cheeks still held a rosy hue of embarrassment, but her eyes blazed. "I just think it would cause unnecessary upset in the town if Old Jamie were killed. Better that he just gets sent on his way."

"You don't have to explain away an act of compassion, miss," Maddileh said. "Kindness on its own is more than enough of a reason."

Saralene stared, clearly taken aback, then smoothed her expression to one of indifference and said, "If you will excuse me, I have tasks to attend to."

Maddileh bowed, this sign of courtesy seeming to confound the servant even more.

She's like me, Maddileh realised as Saralene bustled off, *a woman trying to find her place in a man's world.* But Maddileh wasn't fooled by all this master-and-servant stuff. Saralene's knowledge of magic, her informal way of talking in front of Kennion, made it likely that Kennion was training her up, something that other mages generally frowned upon. There had been female mages in the past, but they didn't number very many and didn't often make it beyond the level of Distinguished Mage. Magic was given to the world by the Allfather, and so was usually within the remit of men alone. From Saralene's attitude, Maddileh couldn't imagine her being a woman to settle for being allowed in the Guild and then kept at a junior level. Perhaps that's why she'd sought out Kennion, a man whose great-grandmother had risen to high acclaim. Who better to fight in her corner against the Guild?

But Maddileh pitied Saralene. She'd met similar women at her father's court, women so fired with ambition that they were constantly dissatisfied with their own station in life, thinking everyone was mocking them for not being more than they were. They had a tendency to believe that behind every smile cast in their direction was a smug satisfaction that they hadn't risen higher. As a child, Maddileh had always wondered whether such women would be happy even if they became empress of all the fourteen realms; she had concluded they would not. Still, despite Saralene's haughtiness, she had tended towards kindness for Old Jamie, so perhaps there was hope for her yet.

Once Maddileh's turn of the room was complete, and all niches and dark corners had been examined, the Knight of the Stairs wandered out into the street and strolled away from the meeting place. She headed towards the late-night market that was still in full flow, constantly checking her surroundings for anyone tailing her. When she was satisfied that no one was following her, she slipped along several dark alleys until she'd made her way back to the hall. Choosing a shadowy vantage spot, she kept watch on those passing the hall, alert for any sidelong glances that might indicate a sly interest in the venue. One man passed by twice in two different directions. While the bundles in his arms during the second pass suggested he'd gone somewhere to buy wares and was now returning, there was something in his manner that suggested his mind was more on his surroundings than his purchases. The strange tilt of his head indicated he was taking surreptitious glances at the hall, and the fact that he paused right in front of it, shifting his packages for a better grip, seemed too staged. She made a mental note of his defining features, then turned her attention to other passersby.

At one point, when Saralene was leaving the hall to fetch something, she was accosted by a group of men laughing outside a tavern. Maddileh had noted and dismissed them earlier, but their interest in the servant made her tense, ready to intervene. Yet Saralene used her stinging rebukes and their sluggish responses to her advantage, slipping past them when they were loudly laughing at their own jokes. Except one of them was not laughing. While the other three called after her, cajoling her to come back, the fourth man in the group watched her go with a mute thoughtfulness that made Maddileh uneasy. She didn't much care for the way the man turned round and looked directly, calculatingly, at the hall, but a few moments later, heavy raindrops started falling from the sky, sending the men inside the tavern, covering their ale with their hands.

Maddileh pressed herself closer to the wall she was leaning against, the overhang of the roof protecting her from the worst of the weather. Ten minutes later, Saralene reappeared and entered the hall, unobserved and unmolested. Another thirty minutes of watching proved unproductive, and then the first mages started to arrive and it was time to take up her station inside the hall.

❀ ❀ ❀

IF MADDILEH WAS honest with herself, she was a little disappointed with how unremarkable the mages' meeting was. Before the job began, she'd imagined them summoning the dead from the underworld, coaxing demons from a roaring fire, or plunging the room into some unnatural darkness. But all they did was eat, drink, talk, and scribble things down on pieces of paper. A few times, voices were raised in argument, but by the time Maddileh had looked in that direction, another mage had already started smoothing away the disagreement.

"I've seen more liveliness in a graveyard," she muttered as Saralene went past; the servant gave her a cold look, but there was a hint of a curve to her lips as if she were trying not to smile.

"Not quite what you expect from mages, is it?"

Later, the servant brought Maddileh a glass of water and an onion tart. "What, none of their fine wines for the likes of me?" Maddileh teased.

Saralene raised an eyebrow. "Well, if I can't have any, then neither can you," she said archly, but with a smile.

Maddileh laughed and bit into the tart. The onions were sweet, and cubes of cheese on the top gave the whole thing a deliciously salty tang. "I thought I'd at least see some magic, though."

"They aren't fairground conjurers," Saralene said, with more warmth and less haughtiness than before. "These men are academics. They talk about the theory of magic. They don't perform tricks. What they're talking about in this room, what they're planning, it will revolutionise magic."

"Not many women here tonight," Maddileh said, trying to keep it conversational but watching Saralene too.

The servant gave her a wry look. "No women here tonight at all, you mean."

"Shame," Maddileh said, chewing and swallowing the last of the tart. "Plan to change that, do you?"

When Saralene glared at her defensively, Maddileh added, "You went into the hall wet from the rain, and then a few moments later, you were dry again. Magic."

"Distinguished Mage Kennion provided the spell," Saralene replied. "You don't think he'd want a sodden servant at his gathering, do you?"

Maddileh grinned.

"I might believe that if I hadn't seen you cast the spell on yourself through the window."

Saralene's eyes widened, then narrowed. "I wasn't anywhere near the window when . . ." Her pause was so slight others might have missed it, but Maddileh saw in her eyes how fast her mind was working. "Distinguished Mage Kennion cast the spell," she finished.

Maddileh said nothing, keeping her grin steady, and Saralene stormed off—or rather, gave the impression she would have stormed off if it wasn't such an undignified thing to do.

Maddileh knew when to leave things well alone and so didn't approach Saralene again or even glance her way. In the end, Saralene came to stand before her, hands on hips.

"I won't tell anyone," Maddileh said before the mage-adept could speak.

This clearly caught Saralene by surprise, and her eyes became sharp, giving Maddileh the impression she was being reassessed.

Eventually, Saralene said, "I'd appreciate that, thank you. It is not an easy position I'm in."

"Yes, I always wondered how it works with women," Maddileh mused. "I mean, there's an absolute prohibition against teaching women magic without special dispensation from a Sub-Grand Mage. But some highborn girls are trained from a young age, showing that money can purchase all sorts of exceptions to the rules. Meanwhile, girls from the middle classes who show an aptitude for it have to present themselves to one of the fourteen Sub-Grand Mages to have their skills tested. Isn't that right?"

"It is."

"Well, that's where I get confused. I mean, it's illegal to train girls in magic without a dispensation, yet to get that dispensation, a girl has to show an aptitude first—which means someone has to train her up at least a bit, which means that someone is already breaking the rules in order to follow the rules. That seems ridiculous to me."

Saralene shrugged. "The rules are centuries old. We can't change them, however much we might want to, but some tweaks over the years have led to . . . inconsistencies, I suppose."

"Well," said Maddileh, gesturing to her scruffy knight's clothes, "you can see that I'm not one who thinks any profession should be barred to women."

With a snort of amusement, Saralene observed, "A disgraced knight is hardly a figurehead for women, is it?"

Maddileh shrugged. "Sometimes, a figurehead doesn't have to be good at what she does—she just has to be."

"Does your disgrace not bother you?" Saralene asked with what appeared to be genuine curiosity.

Maddileh took a long, slow drink of water before she answered. "Yes. Every night, when the world is at its darkest. And I think about how I can fix it at least once every hour."

"Is that what brought you here? To work for Distinguished Kennion?"

"Something like that," Maddileh said evasively. She was growing to like Saralene, but she sensed the woman's sharp tongue would make short work of her audacious plan if Maddileh were to reveal it. So she changed the topic. "I've always been curious—the highborn girls get trained openly, the middling in secret to begin with before they're good enough to be accepted by the Guild, but what about those from the lower classes who show promise?"

"Saralene!" Kennion called out from across the room. "More wine and paper, please!"

The mage-adept moved away to collect the necessary items, and Maddileh thought that her question would go unanswered. But as Saralene passed by again, she slowed and said quietly, "No mage would sully himself to teach a lower-born girl with magical potential, so they are left unchecked. Their power grows, untutored, until it becomes dangerous. That makes them a threat to their kingdom—and what do you do with such a threat?"

"Eradicate it," Maddileh replied solemnly.

Saralene nodded and placed something on the table next to the knight before heading off again. It was a glass of fine wine.

SIX

Time became hazy in the tunnels. Knights were trained to ignore hunger pangs, so Maddileh didn't even have the grumbling of her belly to help her keep track. Not that she felt particularly hungry, she had to admit. When she'd ventured into the lair of the Shimmering Corsair, she hadn't felt hungry because of her state of near-constant panic. She'd been only nineteen at the time, still naive in the ways of knights. But when her experience took her with Sir Alfonso into the demesne of the Silken Sigh, she'd felt all her senses dulled by magic. Perhaps this was something similar, although hunger seemed to be the only sensation missing. Trepidation, excitement, exhaustion—all those churned through her.

She felt the best option would be to stop when Petros got hungry; after all, he looked like a squire who didn't often miss a meal. There was lean muscle on his body, but also a fullness to the cheeks that suggested good living.

To her surprise, before he mentioned a thing about food, a chiming like a dozen little bells came from his pocket. He hurriedly sorted through his jacket, pulling out a tiny orb that was emitting the chimes, little vibrations running through it. He whispered to it, "Rest," and it instantly fell silent. Catching Maddileh's stare, he explained, "It's a chronology orb, a timekeeper. It rings twice a day at noon and midnight, to make sure we don't lose track of time. It's probably a good idea to stop and eat." There came a scrabbling of small claws from the darkness ahead, and Petros added, "Although maybe it would be prudent to—"

"Here will be fine," Maddileh said, swinging her bag onto the ground. She unbuckled her breastplate and set that to one side, luxuriating in the absence of its weight for a moment. She left on the greaves and vambraces, though; unknotting so many leather ties for a short stop was not worth it.

Petros reached into his bag and pulled out a phial that just fitted in the palm of his hand. Opening the top revealed a pipette. With great care, Petros squeezed a single drop onto each item in front of him: a piece of cheese, a thick slice of rough bread, and half a dried apple. Even before he'd stoppered the bottle, the food began to change, bubbles spreading across the surface as if he'd sprinkled acid over it. Each item of food liquified into a puddle, and although the edges of each puddle touched the other, they did not mix. Some sort of vapour was rising from those piles of sludge, and the air became filled with the aromas of freshly baked bread and crisp apples. Two lumps were forming in each puddle, the liquid now creeping back towards the centre. The mounds grew in size and became more distinct with each passing second until all the sludge was gone and the plate held two slices of bread, two hunks of cheese, and two halves of an apple.

"I . . . never saw such a thing," Maddileh said, shocked and a little unsettled.

"Magic can be used for many purposes," Petros said, tucking the phial away again. He offered the plate to Maddileh, but she suddenly felt too queasy to eat. Although the food looked just as it had before, all she could think of was the bubbling sludge it had turned into.

"Thank you, but I have no appetite right now," she said, leaning back against the wall. Petros shrugged, took one of the apple halves, and bit into it.

"You seem very comfortable with magic," Maddileh commented, "more so than most squires I've met. In fact, you're so at home with it, I'm tempted to guess you were a mage-adept before you became a squire."

Petros's eyes narrowed. "Yes, I was an adept, once."

When nothing else seemed forthcoming, Maddileh pressed, "But you left? Or were turned out?"

"No. I was . . . taken aside. Things were explained to me, and I decided to become a squire of my own choice." His words were spoken with a precision of thought that suggested this was all the truth she was likely to get out of him. But it was enough to be going on with, and she was pleased her suspicions about his magical predilections were correct. Perhaps, like she, he'd faced disgrace and collecting some precious item from the dragon would restore his honour. It would make them quite the pair if that were the case.

"Why do you dislike magic so much?" he asked around mouthfuls of bread. "Seems a strange aversion for someone who hunts magical creatures."

"I don't always hunt them."

"Ah, no. Of course not. You used to ride in the tourneys, didn't you?" He spoke with no malice or spite, just a simple statement of fact.

"I did. And now I've decided that I need the Fireborne Blade, and retrieving that, unfortunately, requires magic." She spoke candidly, in a way she would not in the world outside. But spending any time with someone in a dark, cramped space thick with magic, where death lurked at your destination, often bred a feeling of kinship between the un-likeliest of people. "I see its uses, and I have a great respect for mages, but it feels like cheating. At life. At hunting. At archery."

And I've heard of it going wrong too many times to feel happy carrying it around in my pocket.

"Archery?" Petros said, quirking an eyebrow in amuse-ment. A scuffling sounded farther down the tunnel, and Petros's head snapped in that direction, his body tensing.

"Yes, archery." The sound didn't bother Maddileh. It was probably a soot drake. Those little creatures wouldn't try to eat you, except by accident when they were chewing through your soot-covered clothes. They lived by licking the black substance off the walls of dragon tunnels and weren't re-motely interested in human flesh. But if you brushed against the wall and got soot on your clothes, they considered it a feast, and the gums of a drake exuded a necrotising liquid that could turn a person's flesh black then rotten. So they could be dangerous, but they were not to be feared.

The things to be truly terrified of in these tunnels would

make no sound at all. But she could see that Petros was unnerved by the distant noises, and a jumpy squire was a liability, so she settled into storytelling mode, hoping it would distract him.

"My father used to have an annual sports event around midsummer. Squires could go up against knights, farmers could go up against the castle guards—even my father joined in with the wrestling at times. One year, a mage showed up. He fought with an enchanted blade against my brother. There were sparks each time they clashed and a sound like thunder. It was impressive, but it lacked skill. My brother ceded to the mage, who was not a gracious winner."

Petros was watching her, his shoulders slowly lowering as the tension left his body.

"On the log roll, we have a rule against putting anything on your feet to aid grip, but we didn't have a rule about putting anything on the log itself. So the mage threw some kind of net over it that squeezed the wood flat and sucked away the grease. Then he walked over the log as if it were nothing more than a footbridge. It was showy, but no one was impressed.

"When it came to the archery, the crowd was getting miserable. We knew he would win, and he did—with an enchanted arrow. He couldn't even draw the bow properly. It was pitiful. But he still won. He went away laden with trophies and left my father fuming at the injustice of it all."

Petros nodded. "There are some brothers out there who sully the name of mage with cheap trickery or sly manoeuvring. But don't be deceived, Master. There are many mages who follow selfless lives, devoted to study and the good of our kind." As he spoke, a little lizard head popped up from behind his shoulder. The creature was chewing on what looked like a strap from Petros's satchel. Maddileh was already rising to her feet when Petros saw the soot drake. He screeched and jumped into the air, spinning round and shrieking, "Get it off! Get it off!"

Maddileh grabbed him, trying to hold him still. If a soot drake felt threatened, it would dig its claws and teeth into what it was standing on. As Petros twisted and cried out, Maddileh yelled, "If you try to throw it off, it'll bite you. Stay still!"

Petros instantly froze, although he was trembling all over.

Luckily, the soot drake seemed more dazed than frightened. Maddileh took a grubby handkerchief out of her pocket and rubbed it on the wall, covering with soot. Then she dangled it in front of the lizard's nose. "Here you go—take a bite of this." The lizard's tongue flicked out, tasting the offering before it lunged forward and bit down. Maddileh lifted both handkerchief and lizard off Petros's shoulder and dropped them on the floor, where the drake scampered away with its prize.

Petros straightened, trying to control his trembling. "Thank you. I . . . thank you."

"You're welcome. I didn't think we were far enough down for them yet. Still, no harm done."

Petros, who'd been minutely examining his shoulder, let out a breath when he found no puncture marks. "It seems not," he agreed.

As they were gathering up their belongings, Petros asked, "Have you ever had a soot drake bite?"

"No, but I saw a knight with one. It was chewing on his helmet one night and woke him when it bit his ear."

In the strange blue light of the orb, it was hard to be sure, but Petros looked like he'd gone grey. "His ear?"

"Yes. We cut the whole thing off, but it was too late. The poison was already spreading. In the end, my master put a sword through the man's heart, but even dead, that rot kept spreading throughout his body. We had to leave him in the darkness, his corpse slowly turning to something that stank worse than manure."

Petros checked his shoulder yet again. "No harm done," he muttered, although he didn't sound convinced.

SEVEN

THE DEMISE AND DEMESNE OF DRAGONS
Appendix VI
A word about dragon-dead

Revenants in the outside world are, thankfully, a rarity. But those who die within a dragon's lair will find no rest for the soul. Generally, a dragon-dead soul will confine its roaming to the immediate vicinity of the dragon's lair and will be averse to sunlight. One notable exception to this is the demesne of the Silken Sigh, where the dead roamed down into the valley floor itself, forcing those few left living out of the village.

As a rule, dragon-dead will be oblivious to anyone passing by so long as that person makes no sound. Those knights, squires, and mages who have drawn the attention of a ghost might live to regret their mistake, but only for a short time.

During the 713th Year of the Reckoning, the Knight of the Cherry Blossoms fled the lair of the Grey Flux with the soul of a former knight clinging to his back. While Sir Lowick had tried in vain to prise its ghostly fingers from around his neck, they were as insubstantial as mist. Yet he could clearly feel the pressure of them digging into his skin.

When he crawled out into the late-afternoon sun, the ghost released him with a shriek and fled yammering back into the dark of the caves. Sir Lowick spoke later of how he had lain there many moments to allow the fear and trembling to subside, but that he was raised from such recuperation by the hissing taunts of the ghost within the passage. It was lurking there, its gaze intently fixed on Sir Lowick, and the knight was fearful that the phantom might come for him when the sun set.

He was right to be fearful since, as he stumbled down the hillside, the last rays of the sun vanished and the ghost came after him, howling like a demented thing.

Luckily, Sir Lowick met with Lower Mage Lair who had enough amulets on him to cause quite an explosion. The ghost was unharmed but driven away. Lower Mage Lair took the knight back to his hut and tended to his needs. As well as a slight fever and intense dehydration, Sir Lowick had ugly red wheals on his neck from the ghost's fingers.

It was fortunate for Sir Lowick that his uncle was both rich and kindly disposed towards him, because the ghost came for the young man night after night, even when Sir

Lowick was many miles away. The only thing that kept the ghost from claiming its victim was a sigil barrier drawn in essence of violet nightshade. While the plant is widely grown, its distillation is complex and expensive, which is where the uncle's fortune came in. The uncle paid for a constant supply of the essence for the rest of his nephew's life—which was sadly only another three years. While the essence, applied nightly to the forehead, feet, and hands of the afflicted knight, prevented the ghost from claiming his victim, nothing could prevent the dragon-dead from being in the same room as Sir Lowick, and the shade would rage and curse at the young man all night. The experience sent the poor boy quite mad until he refused all food and drink and spent his days weeping.

We are indebted to Lower Mage Lair for obtaining a report of the knight's experiences while he was still comprehensible.

Of course, Sir Lowick's pitiful story is an extreme example. In most reported encounters, questers find the dragon-dead ignore them completely if they are silent and slow in passing. If the attention of a ghost is drawn to an individual, the ghost may reach out and touch the individual. If contact is made, the living person will be infected with nightmares from a period ranging from a few years to the rest of their lives. A full list of tainted individuals and the specifics of their nightmares is included in Appendix XIII, but it should be noted that many of the nightmares involve the tainted individual reliving the ghost's death over and over again as if it were their own.

EIGHT

SIX MONTHS AGO

The mages' meeting had been so dull and uneventful that Maddileh seriously considered finding a shadowy corner to lurk in where she might close her eyes for a bit. Not even the notorious Old Jamie put in an appearance. The only thing of note was that the quiet man from the tavern had come outside at one point to smoke his pipe. No harm in that, of course, but he'd spent his smoking time leaning against the wall, his eyes fixed on the meeting hall. Maddileh had watched him through the window, certain that he couldn't see her thanks to the wards, but with her hand tight on the sword at her belt, just in case. He'd finished his pipe, tapped the bowl against the wall to empty the ash, then returned to the tavern.

It might have seemed innocent enough on the surface, but Maddileh had survived this long as a knight because she paid attention to a person's body language, posture, and details such as whether their eyes darted over you or fixed in one spot. In a sword fight or wrestling, careful observation meant that you could sometimes tell what your opponent was going to do almost the same second that they did. The manner in which the man had stared at the hall had been intense. He had been a man pondering not why but how.

There seemed to be no formal closure to the meeting; the mages just drifted away in ones and twos. Eventually, there was only Kennion, Saralene, and Maddileh left. When the mage addressed Maddileh, his voice was hoarse.

"A most splendid evening and a productive one too. Yes, yes, most productive. Our discussions on the elliptical sources of the lesser runes were most elucidating. I honestly think that—oh, I'm sorry. You're not the slightest bit interested, are you?"

"With respect, Distinguished One, magic interests me only so far as it's necessary to hunt and kill a dragon," Maddileh replied, but she could see the hungry look in Saralene's eyes as the adept glanced their way while tidying up.

"Quite, quite, as it should be."

"But for what it's worth, I'm pleased that it was a successful evening for you. I'm not fond of mages, but the men here seemed . . . different from what I . . ." She stopped because the mage was giving her an amused and penetrating look.

"You are most polite, just as the stories say about you, sir knight."

"Stories?"

Kennion waved his hand dismissively. "We all have stories about us. Now, for your payment, come with me. Saralene, finish up here, will you?"

"Yes, sir."

Maddileh followed the mage out of the hall and back to his lodgings. Kennion's home was large, but the rooms felt cramped because of the shelves lining the walls, stuffed with items and curios. The air was stale with the scent of matches and burnt matter. She waited as Kennion counted out the coins he owed her before, most importantly, writing down the information she needed.

"Thank you again for a most uneventful evening. If you come back in six months, I could guarantee you another night's work, maybe several."

"Thank you, Distinguished One, but I hope to be off hunting dragons by then."

"Of course. Well, good night to you."

Upon leaving the mage's house, Maddileh decided to walk for a while, stretching her legs and clearing her lungs of the musty air. Her thoughts were aimless, but her steps took her in the direction of the hall again. For no reason beyond the fact that her guts were uneasy, Maddileh took up a position in a different shadowy corner and watched the hall. Light through the windows indicated that Saralene was still working inside.

She'd come by her position in a roundabout way, keeping to the back alleys and the shadows. Now she scanned the other alleyways, and in one of them, she felt sure she'd seen a hint of movement.

It was a full twenty minutes before Saralene came out. By that time, the noisy group from the tavern had been kicked out and were standing on the street, laughing, joking, and heckling one another. When they had first come out, Maddileh had been concerned to note that the quiet man was not with them. As Saralene locked the hall, the knight's eyes flicked to the alleyway where she'd seen a shadow lurking. Saralene started down the main road, but upon seeing the three drunks, she altered her course to avoid them—down the alley with the lurking shadow.

With a glance at one another, the three men fell silent, their ebullience turned sinister, and they quickly and quietly followed Saralene into the dark street. Maddileh stepped out of her own hiding place, hurried soundlessly across the road, and proceeded down the alley as well. She spied the group about halfway along, the fourth man with them now, Saralene pressed into the ground. A gag was in the adept's mouth, and she was twisting and thrashing against the men who were knotting ropes around her wrists and ankles.

As Maddileh silently approached, she heard one of the men say, "I still reckon we should turn her into the Mage Guild. They'd give us a pretty penny for her."

"No," snarled the quiet man, his impatience evident. "I told you I already have someone interested in this young lass, and he will pay far better than the Guild. Now, shut up and—"

"Hey, you!" Maddileh called out. As she'd been approaching, she'd pulled a small, glowing marble out of her pocket. As the startled men turned in the direction of her voice, she squeezed her eyes shut and threw the marble at the ground, where it shattered. The burst of bright light turned her eyelids red; the men shrieked and cursed. After opening her eyes, Maddileh's dagger and a blackjack from her belt made short work of the staggering men. In less than a minute, three of them were unconscious on the ground.

Clearly having a greater instinct for self-preservation, the fourth man had stumbled away while Maddileh was subduing the others. She untied Saralene and asked, "Shall I go after him?"

"No. Let him go."

"But he was working for someone. Don't you want to find out who it was?"

"I have a pretty good guess who it was," Saralene said, rubbing her wrists and wincing. Then she turned to the men and muttered a few words while she waved her hands over them.

"What was that?" Maddileh asked when she'd finished.

"Just a stillness spell, to make sure they don't run off before the constables arrive," Saralene said grimly. She was trembling a little, but seemed otherwise composed. Then she looked at Maddileh, and the knight saw the fear in her eyes. "That was . . . I mean, thank you."

Something about the honesty in her voice and the vulnerability in her eyes made Maddileh's heart lurch as if caught by a tiny hook.

"Can you walk?" Maddileh asked.

"Yes, but not too fast, I think."

Maddileh slipped an arm around Saralene's waist, trying to ignore the warmth of the adept's body against her night-chilled hands as they made their way back to Kennion's lodgings.

It had been Maddileh's intention to leave the adept on the doorstep, but Saralene insisted she come inside. She showed Maddileh into a small room with surprisingly comfy chairs before disappearing into the depths of the house. Maddileh settled herself in one of the seats to wait. A few minutes later, she saw a man leaving the house, and she surmised he must be a servant sent to fetch the constables. When a burly pair of men followed a few moments later, Maddileh wondered if Kennion had decided that a swift knife to the throat might provide a better solution than the law.

Eventually, Saralene reappeared in the doorway and said, "The master wants to see you." Maddileh followed her back through to Kennion's study, where the mage had a sincere and lengthy speech prepared on how women were just as valuable as men, how Saralene was an excellent pupil and no risk to anyone, how the less said the better, and so on. Maddileh was pleased to note that he hadn't insulted her by denying that Saralene was his pupil or tried to convince her the attack had merely been some lustful exuberance gone wrong. Since she could report him and Saralene's arrange-ment to the Guild, it showed a level of trust between them that was pleasing.

"Tell me, how much do I owe you for the extra services you rendered tonight?" the mage asked.

"Nothing, Distinguished One. It is part of the knight's code to defend the helpless." She glanced at Saralene, now apparently recovered and standing as imperiously as ever, looking far from helpless, and she changed that to, "Or those who find themselves unfairly outnumbered."

Kennion drummed his fingers on the table, thoughtful. "Even so, I feel it is proper to give you something."

Maddileh knew a bribe when she heard one. Coldly, she

asked, "Are you suggesting that my silence about your little arrangement is only a certainty if it's bought and paid for?"

Kennion looked genuinely surprised at her suggestion, but it was Saralene who answered.

"My master seeks only balance. The core of magic is balance. If we do not keep balance in all aspects of our lives, then we cannot hope to practice magic efficiently." She gave Maddileh a wry smile and added, "You have encountered enough bad mages, I think, to know that we don't give away gifts lightly. What my master offers you is already earned, not payment for anything in the future."

Because of the smile, and because Kennion hadn't shouted Saralene down for speaking on his behalf, Maddileh agreed. The mage brought out a silver ring with an onyx cabochon on it. "Wear this, and it should protect you from unfriendly enchantments."

"Thank you, sir. I consider matters between us balanced." Kennion nodded, pleased, and she took her leave.

That night, before she went to sleep, Maddileh looked at the ring. It was a helpful trinket, certainly, but the real value was the piece of paper in her pocket, the one that would increase the chances of surviving an encounter with the White Lady. She fell asleep, tingling with the anticipation of being one step closer to her goal, and determinedly not thinking about the warmth of a good-looking woman's body against her own on a cold night.

NINE

Everywhere was heat and flame. Her mind told her to scream and run, but it wouldn't respond. Her vocal cords were choked from breathing in the ash of her own burning body, and her legs were now just blackened flesh, clinging to bone.

With a heart-jolting jerk, Maddileh sat bolt upright, fighting hard against the panic of her nightmare. *I cannot die. I will not burn.*

The air was cool, soothing her fevered skin. There was soft sand beneath her; it had not been turned to molten glass by the heat of dragon fire.

I cannot die. I will not burn. Her mantra ran through her mind, the words bringing her calm. She had been into two dragon demesnes, and on each occasion, her fierce determination had seen her through the dark tunnels, past the lingering ghosts, and back out again into the sunlight.

"Bad dream, Master?" Petros asked. He was sitting against the other wall, a loaf of bread on a plate before him.

"Something like that. All knights get them," she said evasively.

With the fear from her dream still lingering in her core, Maddileh watched Petros remove the tiny silver bottle from his bag. After cutting two slices of bread, he unstoppered the bottle and delicately administered a drop to each slice. After an unpleasant intermediate state, the two slices became four; the scent of freshly baked bread lingered in the air.

"I'll have the original two slices," Maddileh said, not hiding her distaste. Petros glanced at her and then duly handed over the two non-magical slices.

"There's no harm to these two," he said, gesturing to the duplicate slices.

"Perhaps not, but I'll stick to the pieces I have." She took a bite of the bread; it was dry and tasteless on her tongue.

"You know, I once saw this potion used on a human," Petros said idly as he chewed his bread. Maddileh's hand stopped halfway to her mouth, half-curious, half-revolted. "It was recorded on one of the library's visual mage orbs, and the result wasn't what the mages had intended at all. The original theory was to try to grow a missing limb. Think of the benefits that could bring to our knowledge of medicines and the body—how glorious battles would be if we could regrow all lost limbs!"

Maddileh put her bread down on the sand, her stomach roiling in queasy anticipation.

"A man who had recently lost his foot was found and agreed to a trial. Mages had accidentally gotten the potion on their skin before with no ill effects beyond a slight rash. There seemed no harm in taking their tests a bit further.

"Previously, when they'd applied it to the shoulder stump of a young girl who'd been born without an arm at all, nothing had happened. So the hope was that if the potion was applied to the space where something had once been or to a wound that might have dead flesh in it, a different effect would be observed.

"The man was an old soldier, and a physick had been obliged to saw his foot off after a wound turned gangrenous. The leg had healed, although the skin was a little raw from his stump. The mages tried a little bit of potion first, and nothing happened. So they tried a bit more and a bit more. No effects were observed, and the test subject reported no sense beyond the coldness of the potion against his skin.

"Then, when almost a whole bottleful had been used by degrees, the soldier started to complain that his stump felt mighty cold. He reached out to rub it, but the mages prevented him. They tried wiping the residue off with a flannel, but the potion had already penetrated his flesh. The man began to panic, to claw at his stump, claiming it was not cold now but burning and itching. Although the mages tried to restrain him, he fought them off and, whimpering, scratched and scratched at his leg until blood coated his hands. Then, before their eyes, the flesh started to turn into sludge. The soldier's skin and insides began to drain out of his body, creating a pile of red, lumpy gloop on the floor.

"The orb captured the sound of him screaming very well. What disturbed me most was how his mouth was still contorted into a silent scream as his lungs liquified. In less than two minutes, the mages had a pile of flesh and organs on the floor. The mess shuddered and started to split, slowly coalescing into two piles of organs. I remember how they steamed with heat. But what struck me most is how you could see both hearts beating, sending ripples through everything around them. There was no body, no skin, no cohesion—and yet those hearts beat.

"I've watched the recording several times, and each time, I'm sure that you can see the sludge shuddering, as if it's trying to pull itself back together, but none of the other mages agree. They think it's just the heartbeat making it move."

"Poor bastard," Maddileh muttered. "I hope they buried him with dignity. Well, what was left of him."

Petros looked at her with curiosity. "Bury him? There wasn't anything like a body to bury. There wasn't anything resembling a man. So they put both sets of organs into storage containers, and now they're held in the library archives."

"Were the hearts still beating when they were put into containers?"

"Yes. Obviously. A pile of dead flesh isn't really worth keeping, is it? You can get that anywhere."

Queasy, and feeling like her opinion of mages had just been reinforced, Maddileh closed her eyes, trying to rid herself of the final traces of panic that the dream and Petros's story had seeded throughout her body.

"What was it about?" Petros asked. "The dream, I mean."

Telling him meant that he might come to the same opinion that she dreaded was true. But even though she might doubt the wisdom of letting Petros squire for her in the first place, he was here and they were marching into danger together. He deserved the truth. "I dreamed I was burning up in a dragon's flame."

"Ah," said Petros in a carefully neutral voice.

She opened her eyes and gave him a cold stare. "It's a common dream for dragon hunters. It doesn't mean anything," she said.

It doesn't mean that I've been touched by a ghost, that I'll carry his death with me forever.

Hating her vulnerabilities, she changed her gaze to her wrist. All her ghost charms seemed to be there. Surely no ghost could have touched her with such protection? But then, some of them were unfamiliar to her, so maybe she'd lost ones she didn't remember. Her fingers traced the most unfamiliar one, the one without a ribbon, willing herself to recall where she'd gotten it.

"If it helps," Petros said softly, "I honestly believe that you will defeat the White Lady."

Maddileh looked up and was surprised to see a sincere expression on his face. This wasn't just a squire's platitude to calm a skittish knight; he honestly believed it.

"Why do you think that?"

"Well, as the prophecy goes, no living man can slay the White Lady, and the trick with prophecies is to figure out the hole in them, to consider not what they're saying but what they're not saying."

Maddileh grinned. "And what it is not saying is whether a woman can kill the old girl."

"Precisely," Petros said before he stuffed the last piece of bread into his mouth. When he'd swallowed, he added, "I know you find yourself in disgrace, Master, but that is only based on the rules of society. The other knights don't like to be shown up by a woman. But you have an excellent reputation, and although other knights might have had more experience with dragons and tourneys, none of them had half such the experience when they were the age you are now."

"Thank you, Petros," she said, feeling a corner had been turned and regretting her earlier distaste with him.

"All part of a squire's duty, sir. Shall we move on?"

❄ ❄ ❄

IT WAS SEVERAL hours later that they met their first ghost. It had been a frustrating afternoon, with the orb leading them down tunnels that came to a sudden dead end or had a chasm too wide to jump across. Irritable at such delays, Maddileh began muttering about the unhelpfulness of magic, her grumblings getting louder until Petros turned around and snapped, "Since you're wearing magical armour and ghost charms, and as I'm carrying your enchanted spear, your complaints seem a little hypocritical," then added, "sir," when Maddileh glared at him.

"I understand that you don't have much experience being a squire," Maddileh said, "but take heed when I say that you do not—do not—speak to your betters that way." She saw the flash of indignation in his eyes when she said betters, but he was wise enough to keep quiet this time.

Remembering his earlier faith in her, and acknowledging that she was in a particularly bad mood, Maddileh softened her tone as she said, "Magic has its place in society, yes, but the greatest mage magic is no better than a conjurer's trick down in a dragon's lair. Mages might weave magic to their will, but dragons exude magic. It runs through their flesh. So, forgive me if I have less faith in mage magic down here than most people do out there." She gestured backward, although, in truth, the outside world might have been in a completely different direction for all she knew at that moment.

Even though he narrowed his eyes, Petros managed an approximation of respect when he said, "If magic is no use against dragons, why are you wearing enchanted armour? Sir."

She gave him a mirthless grin. "Because to a sinking sailor, a bucket with a hole in the bottom is better than no bucket at all. I've heard of magic failing too many times to have complete faith, but it's still better to have some when you're facing a dragon. And if you stick at this game, you will learn that just because something is useful to you, that doesn't mean you have to like it. Like squires, for example." She gave him a meaningful look, then clapped him breezily on the shoulder. He gave a rueful grin.

After that, the tense atmosphere lifted for a while, but when the orb led them down a tunnel that narrowed to the point of impassability, Maddileh gritted her teeth and muttered swear words under her breath. From the corner of her eye, she saw Petros glancing at her but saying nothing.

And so we progress, she thought grimly. But Petros's humility was not to last, and after another half an hour of subvocal grumbling, he turned to her and snapped, "It's just a tool. It isn't sentient. It takes us down the most direct route, and it can't tell if there are obstacles in the way or not."

Maddileh's patience for teaching was at an end, and she cuffed him round the ear. It wasn't a hard blow, but it was one designed to undermine his dignity, as if he were a mere child who'd misbehaved. "I have warned you, boy, about talking back to me."

"I am not a boy! We are of an age!" he snarled at her.

"Age doesn't matter. Station does. I'm a knight, you're a squire—whatever you might have been before. You do as you're told, and you don't answer back."

"I'm a—" he snarled, then broke off, fury clearly boiling beneath the surface.

"You're a what?" she asked. "A highborn squire? An ex-mage? So what? Whatever drove you to become a squire, you are one now, and you will obey. Tell me, if I were a man, would you have answered back in such a way?"

"If any man was as stubborn as you, I'd . . ." He bit back the end of the sentence. She watched him wrestle with his emotions and finally get them under control. "Forgive me, sir, but I find your attitude to magic at odds to my own thoughts."

And that's why I don't like mages—even ex-mages are all puffed up with their own importance.

"When you are no longer in my employ, feel free to enter into a discussion about the benefits of magic or any other area upon which we disagree. But while you are my squire, while we are down here, you do as I say. And if I want to cuss about magic, I will do." She tapped the map. "Mark down this tunnel and let's go."

Still glaring, Petros marked the dead-end route and instructed the orb to find a new way. Obediently, it turned and floated back the way they'd come, illuminating a man standing facing the wall.

Maddileh stopped dead, reaching out to grab Petros's arm; while stuffing the map back into his pack, he hadn't seen the ghost ahead. He turned at her touch, and she pointed at the ghost. Beneath her fingers, his muscles tensed. His bravado melted away to be replaced by fear.

Is that . . . ? He mouthed the words rather than speaking them; she nodded. Petros couldn't prevent a terrified squeak leaving his lips. The ghost didn't turn round, but his head, which had been angled down, lifted slightly.

Maddileh put a finger to her lips, and Petros nodded. The dragon-dead were unaware of the world around them, and some of them even seemed to be unaware that they were dead. It was possible to slip past them if you were quiet. Hopefully, this one would be sluggish.

As Petros took his first few steps, his bag swung against his leg, and something inside it shifted with a clunk. The ghost's head raised higher, and he seemed to gain an aura of alertness that had been lacking before. Petros winced and pressed his hands against the bags, pinning them to his thighs so they wouldn't move again. Sweat was running down his neck, and his jaw was tight as if his teeth were clenched. Maddileh had the urge to place a comforting hand on his shoulder, but Petros looked like he might scream at the slightest unexpected touch.

Even though Maddileh wore armour, they were single pieces of metal tied on with leather thongs preventing clanking as she moved. Still, she walked slowly and carefully, dividing her attention between Petros, her own footsteps, and the ghost. Once Petros had passed the man, he began to speed up. Maddileh bit down on the inside of her lip, resisting the urge to call after him. He was being an idiot; they needed to be slow, steady, and silent until they were at least a hundred paces away. His fear was making him reckless and was likely to draw down the very thing he was afraid of.

The silence was shattered by the ringing of tiny bells; no death knell had ever sounded so charming. Petros spun round, his eyes wide as he scrabbled inside his pocket for the chronology orb. It seemed as if the noise went on for an age, but it couldn't have been more than a few heartbeats. Petros had the orb in his hand, bringing it to his lips, when the ghost flew at him. Normal ghosts had no substance to them, but dragon-dead were different. When listless, they could pass as easily through stone as air; but when roused, when aware of prey nearby, a dragon-dead ghost could take on a physicality almost as solid as a real person. The ghost cannoned into Petros, knocking him off-balance and sending them both tumbling to the floor. Maddileh closed her eyes just as the ghost had his hands at Petros's throat. The surge of light turned her eyelids bright red; she kept them closed for a count of ten, but even so, her night vision was shattered, replaced by dancing images of light.

Blundering forward as best she could, she found Petros lying on the floor, panting heavily. The ghost was gone.

"Your wrist," Maddileh said. Petros lifted his arm to see

a ring of blue flames where his shade bracelet had been. Crying out with a new fear, Petros stuck his hand into the sandy floor, pouring sand over his wrist until the flames were smothered. Then he laid his head back, panting and trembling.

The chronology orb, which had been chiming merrily away through all this, suddenly fell silent, the last echoes dancing away down the corridor. Petros turned his head, looking dazedly at her.

"Midnight," she said.

TEN

THE DEMISE AND DEMESNE OF DRAGONS

Sir Gaius and Sir Kevan went up against Bluescale when the beast was around one hundred years old. We have no fixed date for their quest, but we estimate it to be around two hundred years from the Reckoning. Its demesne was a warren of tunnels outside Killinghall. The Knight of Greenwater and the Knight of the Cups had two squires with them, whose names have been lost in history (although research by General Mage Kale suggests that one boy might have been Dwight, the fifth son of Roland Sanwell).

It seems that the two knights were either unaware of the dangers posed by sleeping dragons or were too reckless to take heed. Certainly, they lived in an age before we had a great wealth of dragon lore, so perhaps they were just ignorant of what we take as common knowledge today.

In any event, the visual mage orb that Sir Gaius took with him shows what happened in blurry detail.

The two knights spread out so that Sir Kevan is standing by the base of the beast's skull and Sir Gaius is before the sleeping dragon's mouth. The squires seem to be hanging back at the lair entrance as if they somehow think this is safer.

Sir Kevan takes quite some time in angling his sword so that it will slide in beneath the scales. This shows that they did at least know that a dragon's neck is one of its most vulnerable spots. To allow the dragon to twist and turn its long neck, the scales are spaced slightly farther apart on the upper dermis. It appears that the two knights are grinning, evidently drunk on their own bravado.

When Sir Kevan is happy with his angle, he nods to Sir Gaius, who raises his own sword. Then Sir Kevan plunges his sword into Bluescale's neck.

The dragon instantly opens its eyes and bellows. As soon as it jaws gape wide, Sir Gaius plunges his sword into the roof of Bluescale's mouth, burying the blade up to the hilt so that the tip must be lodged deep in the brain. The dragon convulses two times, then expires.

It should be noted that while the two knights showed immense stupidity and breathtaking recklessness (as borne out by missives from their preparations), they were not lacking in courage. To stare a dragon in the eye, then reach your arm into its mouth, braving foul vapours and fierce flames, to lodge a sword in its gullet is something that even the most courageous of knights has shirked in their time.

With the dragon dead, the knights go to embrace each other, and it's possible to hear joyful voices (although it's not possible to make out the words) as the squires run into the cave proper. Then Bluescale explodes, the orb filling with bright white light for the space of seven slow heartbeats. When the scene gradually fades back, the last glimmers of the dragon's death make it possible to see the roof of the cave collapsing. In less than a minute, the cave becomes the inside of the mountain. But what is curious is that while the rockfall is utterly silent, tricking the viewer into thinking the orb's sound function has been compromised, once the rocks have settled and the orb is buried in blackness, the sound of weeping is clearly audible. It is impossible to tell whose voice it is; several mages over the years have listened carefully for clues, but none have been successful (see Table IIB in Appendix VII for their individual assessments).

The weeping continues for two hours, fifteen minutes, and twenty-six seconds, ending only when the orb—fractured by the cave-in—finally ceased working. It had lain there for two hundred years until a shepherd noticed it sticking out from the side of a valley. Its presence there remains a mystery that even the High Mage cannot fathom. It should have been buried at least a mile underground, and simple land erosion would not account for it being so near the surface.

Although descendants of Sir Gaius and Sir Kevan have dug up portions of the valley in the hope of finding the bones of their ancestors, their search has so far been unsuccessful.

ELEVEN

Maddileh knew she needed to judge their rest stops accurately. While Petros looked exhausted, it was clear that he was also still on edge about his run-in with the ghost. Only when his shoulders slumped, his feet scuffed the sand, and his eyes lost their frightened gleam did she declare that they would rest. Without either agreement or protest, Petros let his satchels fall to the floor, then slumped down, hunching over his knees.

Kneeling next to him, Maddileh opened one of the three bags he carried, thinking it was the one that held their food. And while she was correct, as she lifted out a loaf of bread, something beneath it glinted a brilliant sea green in the light from the orb. Curious, Maddileh pushed aside the other rations and saw enough to deduce that it was a decent-sized jade bowl that would fit comfortably in her palm if she stretched out all her fingers. She also had time to see that it had a lid on it before Petros snatched the bag away from her.

"It's a squire's duty to make his master's meals. You must let me do it, sir. I *must* be of use." Maddileh was unable to tell whether his frantic manner was because of his earlier scare or a worry that she'd seen the bowl.

Gently, she said, "I know that, but I thought I would help

you, just this once. You don't look well enough to even hold a spoon steady." His mouth opened and closed as if he kept lining up then dismissing responses. In the end, she said, "But I'm not hungry, so feed yourself if you are, but don't worry about me. This once, it can be squire before master."

Petros looked down at the bag he clutched to his chest. "I'm not hungry either." He placed the bag on the floor but, Maddileh noticed, on the other side of him, away from her. His hands were shaking.

"Here." Maddileh pushed up her sleeve, undid one of the ghost charms, and held it out to Petros. "I told you that a braid was only good for one ghost, even if it was created by the High Mage himself. You can have one of mine."

After glancing at her wrist and the remaining charm bracelets, he took the one she offered. "Thank you. I . . . I didn't think that . . ." He fell silent while he tied it to his wrist, as if speaking one thing and thinking another was too much for him to cope with. "You have another four bracelets. What happens if we meet more ghosts than that?"

Maddileh shrugged. "Then I guess one of us is either having nightmares for the rest of their life or giving a ghost a piggyback ride out of here." Petros shuddered. "But I don't think that will happen. Silent. Steady. Stealthy. Follow those three rules and you'll make it past every ghost we encounter without using up another bracelet."

"Silent. Steady. Stealthy. Yes, I knew the rules, I just . . ."

Maddileh allowed the silence to stretch for a while, then said, "You're not really here to act as my squire, are you?"

Petros's head snapped up, his eyes suddenly alert. "What makes you say that?"

"You don't have any of the basic skills or qualities I see in squires, and I've met a lot of them in my time. You carry my spear in the wrong place. You have a food replication potion—the cost of which is beyond what a squire could afford, and I certainly didn't purchase it. The same with the orb of direction. You've used up precious ration space to bring some kind of green bowl that practically glows with enchantment. You have a bracelet from the High Mage himself, and you place far too much faith in magic, despite no longer being an adept. Squires have a love of action, and their faith lies in steel and swift feet, not in magic. You're all wrong, Petros, and I don't think you're really in the business of squiring. So, if that's the case, then you must be here for another reason. What is it?"

Petros looked down, fiddling with the shade bracelet. "It's rather . . . embarrassing. My sister has been kidnapped by the White Lady, and I need to get her back."

Maddileh was taken aback. "Kidnapped? Really? She's not been"—Maddileh licked her lips, uncomfortable with the bluntness—"eaten?"

"No. Kidnapped. She is alive. I made her a gift of a necklace, an old family heirloom. I didn't know it was enchanted. It drew the dragon right to her. She should be safe, so long as she doesn't take it off or leave with it. My sister has a little knowledge about magic, so she should be able to figure that out at least." There was a hint of snideness in his voice, an indication that Petros didn't approve of magic within women. Maddileh briefly thought of Saralene and wondered what kind of sparks would fly if the two of them ever met. "I'm sorry I deceived you, I just—"

A scream—high, agonised, human—echoed down the tunnel. Petros pressed himself against the wall, the whites of his eyes showing as his head moved left and right, trying to fix the source of the sound.

"It's a disembodied," Maddileh said. "It's just a voice. It can't hurt you like a ghost."

The scream came again—louder, closer—and Petros looked like he'd claw his way through the wall if he could. "I've heard of them," he said, his voice thick with fear. "And I heard some in the mage orbs, but in real life, in the tunnels, I never thought—" He clamped his hands over his ears, squeezing his eyes shut as the sound curled around them, as close as if the man who made it were dying on the floor right next to them.

Gritting her teeth, Maddileh let the sound wash over her, reminding herself that someone else had died and it was not she.

I cannot be afraid. I will not be afraid.

Two more screams sounded as the disembodied passed them and moved off down the tunnel.

"As unpleasant as it is," Maddileh said, "a disembodied is a good thing. The noise keeps the ghosts away."

Petros, who was now ashen-faced and trembling again, said, "There is no way you can tell me that voice is a good thing."

Maddileh let a few minutes pass, then said, "I often find a story makes the dark seem less oppressive."

"I'm not a child in the nursery to be soothed by fairy tales," Petros snapped. His glare irked her and sapped away the last of her pity.

"As you please, then," she said curtly, making herself comfortable against the wall and closing her eyes. Some distance away now, the scream sounded again.

"What kind of story?" Petros said, just as Maddileh was dozing off.

"What kind did you want?"

"Any. So long as it's nice. With no death or screaming."

Maddileh thought for a moment. "How about the brothers and the Fireborne Blade?"

"Yes, if you like. I haven't heard that in a long time," he replied, relief in his voice. "And it's quite apt, I suppose."

Maddileh sat up, ensuring that a ridge of stone dug uncomfortably into her back to keep her awake. She was getting so weary she might well fall asleep while talking.

"Ages past, the dragons were more than they are now. They were smarter, they could talk, they had songs that told their history, and their tears could impart empathy.

"The stories say that one dragon shared his tears with a princess in the hope she could convince her father to peace between the two races."

"I know that tale," Petros said. "They claimed she was mad and hanged her. I've seen her thigh bone in the High Mage's palace. It has runes carved on it, and it was said to draw out the madness of King Orion when he held it."

Although it annoyed Maddileh to be interrupted, talking seemed to calm Petros, so she let him prattle on for a while until a distant scream caused his words to dry up.

"Shall I continue?" she asked. He nodded mutely. "Dragons and humans have always been enemies—both love gold too much. But there came a time when humans had a new enemy: the Dread Beast. No one knows what it was. Some say it was night terrors made of flesh, others that it escaped from a mage's nightmare. On moonless nights, it would stalk you and rend you limb from limb with savage claws, but if you tried to defend yourself with a sword or a dagger, the blade would pass right through the creature as if it were mist.

"No knight could stand against it, and many of the best warriors in the land died trying to protect the realm.

"Then, one night, a Lower Mage had a vision. No one took him seriously at first since he'd only been at the Guild for a few years."

"Three years."

"If you say so. But eventually, all other options had been exhausted and the High Mage called this terrified boy before him. The boy said that the Dragon Smith could forge a weapon to defeat the Beast.

"It was decided that the best of warriors would be sent as envoy to the dragons. Unfortunately, the best warrior, Sir Drummond, was also the most arrogant, and it was only his flag of parlay that saved his skin from being roasted by the dragon elders for the disdain and rudeness he showed them.

"Other knights—even kings, even the High Mage

himself—tried to reason with the dragons, but their pleas fell on deaf ears. While the dragons despised the Beast too, they were pleased it was killing their sworn enemy.

"Then one night, Sir Drummond's little sister, Livia, slipped away from her father's castle, and, on his best horse, she rode to the demesne of the dragon elders. She had no flag of parlay and might have been eaten alive by the guards except that one dragon, Esmerith, prevented them.

"'What manner of human are you to come into our cave with no weapon, no flag, and no sigils of power?' she asked Livia. 'I'm a girl,' was the reply, 'and I bring you this.' 'What is it?' asked the dragon. 'It is a corn dolly, to bring you luck,' the child replied.

"Esmerith stared, and then she laughed so hard the rocks themselves trembled. 'Foolish child! What care we dragons for corn and harvests, except that it makes you and the beasts of the field fat for our bellies?' Livia wasn't afraid. Instead, she frowned. 'But my father told me that dragons value only the most priceless treasure, and this is my most treasured possession. My mother made it for me, the year before she died. She said it would bring me luck, and whenever I look at it, I think of her. I can offer you nothing more precious.'

"When she heard this, Esmerith felt her scorn wither within her, replaced by pity for the child. 'Indeed you are a bold child, Livia, and a wise one. Come, let us see if my brothers and sisters will speak with you.'

"Esmerith took Livia before the other elders, who raged and fumed at the insult of being sent a little girl as a negotiator. 'Please, sir,' Livia said to the eldest dragon, 'no one sent me. I came by myself.' That answer intrigued the dragons enough for them to hear her. She told of the fear of her family behind their stone walls; she told of the terror of the villagers behind their wooden doors; and she told of the silences of their animals in the fields, who knew they had no walls or doors to protect them from the Dread Beast. She pleaded for the whole realm, and Esmerith was moved to tears by her compassion.

"Turning to the other elders, Esmerith said, 'She is not our enemy—she is a child. The king came to plead on behalf of his subjects, men and women he's never met. He was pleading only for his throne. The knights who came pleaded only for their glory. And the High Mage, for all his fine words, was asking us to save his power. But young Livia pleads for those she meets every day, whether they are lowly, highborn, or animals in the wild. We should help them. I would see no innocent human child die in the same way I would see no innocent child of our kind die. And be sure, brothers and sisters, that if the Dread Beast bores of killing humanity, it will come after us and our own children next.'

"The dragons argued some more, but in the end, they all saw the sense of what Esmerith said, and agreed. While Esmerith, Tito, and Alai went into the depths of the earth with the Dragon Smith—a human who'd sworn to serve the dragons—to create the Fireborne Blade, Livia stayed with the other dragons and learned their ways. It took a full turn of the moon for the sword to be crafted, and then Esmerith presented it to Livia. 'Give this to your best and brightest warrior, and tell him that the luck of all dragon-kind goes with it. But when the Beast is dead, you must bring the sword back. A weapon such as this must not fall into the wrong hands. It has been forged by dragon fire and kissed by one of the Bloodless Princes, imbued with death to all who feel the bite of its blade. The only one immune is the one who wields it.'

"They sent Livia home on a dragon with an honour guard of another four dragons. Arriving in such a manner, her father could not fail to listen to her story. She told him of the Blade and how it must go to the best and the brightest. Sir Drummond naturally stepped forward to take the sword, but while the crowd cheered, Livia moved back. She would not give him the sword, and with five dragons at her back, no one was going to take it from her. Instead, she chose her older brother Marl, the middle child. Marl took it and rode out, accompanied by the dragons. He fought hard, as did the dragons by his side. Four of them died, and Marl was close to his own death too when he finally managed to plunge the sword into the heart of the Beast. It died in a howling fury of poisonous ichor, and Marl might have perished too if the final dragon hadn't wrapped its wings around him to protect them both. With this act of bravery and compassion, the dragon lost its ability to fly because the Beast's foul liquids ate through its wings down to the bone.

"When Marl and the dragon returned, there was joy and feasting, and Marl was arrayed in much splendour. But while everyone else rejoiced, there was one who did not:

Drummond. He still burned at the fact his little brother had won all the glory that should rightfully be his. He coveted the sword more than anything, and he plotted to steal it.

"As both revenge and diversion, Drummond cast Livia from the highest tower to her death. While those in the castle crowded around her broken body, he strode into the armoury and seized the Fireborne Blade. Esmerith had known that any blade that dispatched the Beast would be tainted by its evil. A warrior pure of heart, like Marl, could have withstood the greedy, cruel thoughts that crept into his mind, but Drummond was instantly besotted with them. He rampaged through the castle, killing all in his path, even his own family. When the last of the dragon guard tried to stop him, Drummond slew the noble beast too.

"After that, he ventured forth, intending to spread a plague of violence and looting over the realm. For the span of almost three moons, he achieved his goal, and his name became synonymous with fear.

"But then, one day, a farmer found his headless corpse in a nearby ruin. His body was a charred mess, but his armour remained bright and shining; even his clothes were intact. No one could fathom how every inch of the man's flesh might have burned up without his clothes being so much as singed.

"In addition, the Fireborne Blade was gone. The villagers nearby whispered that they'd seen a great dragon fly over their houses one dark night; some said it had clutched the blade in its talons, while others declared that a figure sat atop the dragon, wielding the sword, which flashed with the light of the moon. Legend says that Esmerith retrieved the blade and hid it away within the bowels of the world. The dragons either couldn't destroy it or feared to do so, because that might release the evil inside. Since then, it has become a myth that knights and squires tell around the campfires, each dreaming that they might be the one to finally find it, to wield it with glory because their heart is pure."

Silence fell between them. Petros had lost his hunted look and now appeared merely pale and drawn. He looked, for all his height and long limbs, like a child exhausted from the day. Maddileh suddenly ached for her baby brothers, left behind in her father's stronghold. The twins had been an unexpected addition to her family, but a welcome one, and on stormy nights, Maddileh would sneak into their nursery and tell them stories to make the thunder seem less frightening.

"So, you believe it exists?" Petros asked, his words a little slurred.

"Perhaps. Perhaps not. But if it does, the White Lady has it, and I'll find it. They say she's so old she might even have been alive in the time of the elders, when dragons were smart, before they became nothing more than greedy, instinctual beasts. Maybe I'll find it, maybe I won't. But if I can bring anything back from her lair, if I can kill her, then that will be glory enough."

Petros closed his eyes. Maddileh did the same, but just as the fuzziness of sleep was creeping into her mind, the distant sound of weeping snapped her eyes open once more. Her first instinct was to look at Petros, but he was lying down, his chest rising and falling regularly. Tilting her head and closing her eyes to cut out other distractions, Maddileh determined that the sobbing was coming from down the tunnel to her right.

"Petros?" she whispered.

"Yes?"

"I can hear sobbing. Can you?"

A pause, then, "No. Maybe. Who cares? It's far away."

Maddileh listened harder. Ghosts made no sounds; soot drakes gave reptilian squeaks. It could be a disembodied, of course, but there was a solidity to it that seemed to belie such an origin.

"Could it be your sister, do you think?"

Petros gave a snort of laughter. "My sister doesn't cry, not even after being kidnapped by a dragon."

Maddileh lay in the gloom, listening to the sobbing. Soon, she heard Petros's soft snores and wondered at a man who could sleep through the sound of such sorrow.

Eventually, the sound died away, and Maddileh finally allowed her eyes to close, welcoming sleep but dreading the dreams it would bring.

TWELVE

THE DEMISE AND DEMESNE OF DRAGONS
Figure 26.A.II. The Armour of Sir Wragg, Knight of the Little River

In the 725th year since the Reckoning, Sir Wragg traveled to the demesne of the Malice. It is unclear what happened within the marsh caves, because not only did Sir Wragg take no mage orbs, but once the Malice died, the magic holding back the marsh water from its caves dispelled rapidly and its lair was flooded.

The villagers described to Distinguished Mage Levis how the ground had shaken so violently that many items of furniture fell to the floor and, in one case, a chimney collapsed. It is unclear whether this was due to the Malice's demise or its fight with Sir Wragg.

An eel man called Artur braved the stormy sky the next morning to catch eels for his pot, and he saw something glinting and steaming in the distance. Upon discovering it was Sir Wragg, grievously injured, Artur hauled the knight back to the village. He did this to much personal detriment since he lost two fingers in the process.

A physick was called from a nearby town, and he arrived just in time to witness Sir Wragg die. His written report, shown to the writer of this chronicle by Lord Mendive (Sir Wragg's father) reads as follows:

Even before I reached my destination, I could hear the poor boy's screams of agony. It was as if the marsh itself was crying out in sympathy. Upon attending the patient, I noted that his armour had three large and half a dozen small holes in it. The edges of the holes were blistered and bubbling, and I decided that the knight had come into contact with some acid that was eating away the metal. As the armour dripped onto his skin, that too began to bubble and burn. In two of the three holes, I could see down to his ribs.

I urged the villagers present to help me get his breastplate off him. While I wished at the time that they'd taken Sir Wragg's armour off already, I am now convinced that doing so would not have saved him; the acid had eaten too far into him. I understand that none of them tried to do so after they saw how acid had gotten onto Artur's own skin and badly burned two of his fingers.

With their help, and the aid of several eel glaives and iron pokers, we managed to lever off the armour with no

harm to ourselves but with great damage to the metal im-
plements where they touched the acid. After examining the
wounds, taking note of his humours, finding the young
man pale, and being unable to find any way to remove the
acidic spheres of armour from his wounds, I realised I could
do nothing more for the poor boy except ease his passage to
the next life. I gave him some opiates to ease the pain, but
that gave him only a few minutes' respite before the acid
ate through to his lungs and he suffocated.

It grieves me greatly, my lord, to bring you such dis-
tressing news. I wish I could say that the young man died
painlessly, but you asked me in your letter to be honest and
frank. I can say that he spent his last hours with friendly
voices and soothing words all about him, and he perished
with all the courage of a true warrior. Furthermore, he was
able to kill the dreadful Malice—something for which the
marsh folk esteem him greatly. In fact, I stayed a few nights
with them, and every night, each home raised a toast to
your son's name, and I believe they still do.

If I might, I wish to add that Artur Waterage is now
unable to practice his trade anymore owing to the injuries
he sustained while rescuing your son. It is not my place to
counsel a lord, but I would beseech you to look kindly on the
man and his family, and perhaps compensate them in some
way for their losses.

It would seem from local and genealogical records that
Lord Mendive provided Artur Waterage with enough
money to set up an inn, which the former eel man named

the Blistered Prince. Although Sir Wragg was not a prince, the name corroborates the physick's assertion that the young knight was something of a hero to the marsh folk.

The inn still stands today, and the landlady is proud of an eel pie recipe that, legend has it, Lady Mendive's cook provided at her mistress's insistence.

Water samples taken in the area indicate a slight acidity, but nothing too unusual for a marsh. There are tales that now and then treasure from the flooded caves floats to the surface, but none has done so recently. When Lower Mage Zell visited, one of the villagers showed him a metal teapot that had washed up on the bank and had apparently belonged to the woman's great-great-grandmother. She was particularly pleased to get it back after all these years.

Attempts to send a guided visual mage orb into the depths of the marsh have resulted in images of nothing but blackness.

The remains of Sir Wragg's armour are on display in the King's Armoured Hall.

Thirteen

THREE MONTHS AGO

Maddileh looked at the armour on the dummy before her. Consisting of a breastplate, greaves, and vambraces, it was simple yet beautiful, with scrollwork around the edges and a mirror shine. A dragon's head was etched onto the breastplate, fierce yet elegant. But she knew not to be deceived by beauty. The finest lance on the field can be the first to break.

"Impressive craftsmanship," she said, "but your price is still too high for looks alone. Show me what it can do."

"Of course," said Fain, a man who had the beady eyes and quick motion of a ferret. Maddileh would never have trusted the man if Kennion hadn't provided his name personally. But a mage's word that an armourer's wares were as magical as he claimed they were was worth believing. Still, a demonstration would help convince her.

"Dursa!" Fain called. "Fetch the dragon breath." One of several apprentices—their features indistinguishable beneath the dirt of the forge—ran forward with a bag while another one pumped bellows to heat the fire. A third attached the dummy to a hook suspended from the ceiling; a few tugs on a pulley had armour and dummy suspended over the forge.

Maddileh's eyes flicked over the fabric beneath the metal; it seemed unscorched.

"Watching?" Fain asked with a sly smile before throwing a handful of turquoise powder onto the flames, which leaped up in a roaring inferno. The armour and dummy within it were engulfed. Everyone in the forge turned their faces away from the heat; both Maddileh and Fain had to take a step back. Then the flames died back to plain orange fire.

The stones around the firepit were molten, oozing into new shapes. The chain had snapped so that the armour lay in the fire now. Both the steel and the fabric dummy were unharmed.

There was no sound in the forge beyond the ticking of cooling metal and stone. Maddileh took out a purse bursting with coins—a fortune, but worth it.

FOURTEEN

"Is that . . . ?" Petros asked.

"Yes," Maddileh whispered. "And can you see the ones beyond it?" The glow from the orb drifting ahead of them revealed that what they had thought was a boulder was actually a hunched man on the floor, his knees drawn up and his head buried in his arms. When Maddileh and Petros had halted, the orb had also floated to a stop, far enough ahead that they could make out the definite form of another man and the suggestion of a third one farther on.

Petros let out a shaky breath that was far too loud. Maddileh tensed, her hand going to her sword on instinct, even though it wouldn't do any good. None of the ghosts so much as twitched.

"Just keep quiet," she whispered, "and we'll be fine."

"How many more do you think there are?" Fear lent a harshness to Petros's whisper.

"None? A hundred? I don't know. We'll only find out the truth as we go. Now—"

"Give me another one of your charms," Petros said, turning and pointing to her wrist. Reflexively, Maddileh drew her arm back. "Come on. You don't need them—" Petros stopped short, not meeting her gaze. "I mean you don't need that many of them. I only have one."

"Yes. One I already gave you," Maddileh said with uncharacteristic coldness. "It's not my fault that you came with only one that was used up."

"But the High Mage said . . . Look, just one more, all right?"

Maddileh hesitated. She wasn't a cruel or petty person, and while she disliked Petros, she didn't wish him a lifetime of nightmares or, worse, a ghost living in his skull. But his request and lack of preparation irritated her. What kind of mage goes willingly into a dragon's lair knowing so little?

His sister was captured. Maybe he had to act quickly and didn't have time to prepare. And yet Petros's self-assurance and the careful manner he employed in everything from preparing food to laying himself down at night spoke of a man who didn't rush into anything, not even for a sister.

But the bottom line was: if he stupidly caught the attention of another two ghosts, did she really want his death on her hands when she could so easily prevent it? And he was right in a way, damn him—she didn't need all these bracelets. She'd only ever once needed them against a dragon-dead, and that had been on her first expedition. Since that first terrible encounter, she'd stuck to the rules and never needed protecting again. The number of charms was just insurance in case her luck or stealth ever ran out.

Besides, she thought with cold logic, *if he's stupid enough to attract the attention of a ghost, all I have to do is keep out of the way.*

"Very well," she replied reluctantly, reaching to undo a charm bracelet.

"Not that one!" Petros said loudly enough to make the dragon-dead closest to them shift. In a lower voice, he said, "That one's got no ribbon—it can't be a shade bracelet." He pointed at one with a green ribbon running through it. "Green is my family colour. Please, that one. Please."

Maddileh frowned. *You'll get what you're given.* But Petros was jumpy enough as it was; she worried that if she agitated him further, the resulting outburst might draw a whole host of dragon-dead to them.

"Fine," she said curtly, undoing the green one and handing it over. He snatched it eagerly, muttering a vague thank-you as he affixed it to his wrist. When it was secure, he looked much calmer, even though his eyes flicked covetously to her other bracelets.

The two of them moved slowly and quietly. Whether it was the security of an extra charm bracelet or the concentration required with each step, Petros seemed calmer. They passed shape after shape hunched on the floor; Maddileh stopped counting after thirty. Now and then she would glance over her shoulder, half expecting to see dragon-dead pursuing them with blank eyes and outstretched arms. But she saw only blackness, which wasn't particularly reassuring.

I cannot die. I will not die.

There was a mustiness to the air that dried her throat and made her nose itch.

I will not sneeze. I cannot sneeze.

Their pace was torturously slow, but eventually, she realised they hadn't passed a hunched body for around fifty paces, and her spirits started to lift. She peered ahead, around Petros, and saw that nothing was looming ahead either. After counting another fifty paces, she placed a hand on Petros's shoulder. He jumped, badly startled, but to his credit, he did not make a sound. "They are behind us now. We can talk again, but softly," she said.

He glanced down the tunnel and nodded, but still kept his silence.

By Maddileh's guess, they had been walking for another hour when Petros's bag suddenly started to glow. "What is it? What's happening to your bag?" Maddileh asked, backing away.

"Don't worry. It's just the chronology orb," he said, reaching into his bag. A moment later, the glow vanished. "I issued it with new instructions to glow rather than make a noise. It's midnight. We should rest."

"Good idea," Maddileh said, although sleep was the last thing she wanted. The idea that she might dream about being burned alive for yet another night set a deep cold in her bones. She declined any food, hoping that an empty belly might keep her from falling into a truly deep sleep. Her efforts were in vain, though, because she slipped into a fiery slumber anyway, then awoke, panicked, to blackness.

It took awhile for the afterimage of her own blazing eyelids to fully fade. Only then did she appreciate that the darkness around her was absolute.

Surely the damn orb hasn't gone out? she thought. *Bloody mage magic.* She shifted position, and a new terrifying knowledge descended on her: all sounds were muffled. She ran her fingers through the sand, scraped the wall with her dagger, spoke aloud—all of it sounded like her ears were filled with water, each paltry sound more diminished than the last.

My eyes have failed. My ears too. Gods, what will be taken next? She tried to focus, to remember her training. She took and released several deep breaths that were as silent as the grave.

I cannot die. I will not die—not here, not like this.

"Petros?" She knew she'd spoken the word, had felt the breath tickling across her lips, but her ears picked up nothing. "Petros!" It came out as a silent scream.

Keep calm. Find him. Either he'll be scared and need your reassurance or else he'll know what's going on. With exceptional care and infinite slowness, Maddileh started crawling towards where she'd last seen the young man. After each move forward, she swept the area ahead of her with her hands in an arc. Images of crawling unsuspectingly into a ghost plagued her mind, along with the thought that a soot drake might even now be eating her clothes and burrowing into her skin without her realising it. Would touch be the last thing to go? What if the soot drake ate all the way to her heart and she didn't feel a single thing until the final bite?

Keep calm. You cannot die here. You will not.

Her hand connected with a boot, and then another hand clamped on her wrist. She screamed and tried to back away, but with surprising strength, the hand drew her closer. Just as she was about to twist out of her captor's grip, she felt a hand touch her head. She tugged backward, but the hand followed, moving across her hair, and it took her a moment to realise that it wasn't trying to grab her hair for some nefarious reason—it was stroking her soothingly.

Maddileh went utterly still, her mind racing. *Is it Petros? It must be. Who else is down here—no, don't think of an answer to that question. It's better to ask: Who else other than Petros would work to calm you down? It must be him, yes.* Yet when she brought an image of her companion to mind, she couldn't picture him stroking her hair. If he meant it to be soothing, it wasn't working; her flesh prickled and went tight everywhere the hand touched.

As if sensing her thoughts, the hand moved away from her. A second after, she felt fingers slipping between her own; Petros was holding her hand. It made her think of when her brothers were little and one of them was woken by nightmares; she'd sit by his bed, holding his hand until he fell back to sleep. The memory calmed her, allowing her to find common sense and logic again.

It must be Petros. He's the only thing down here who doesn't mean you harm. If he's so calm, he must be able to see and hear—or at least he's not worried that he can't. This will pass. Don't panic. Are you going to let a mage show you up? No. Good. Just wait this out. The darkness descended, but it will lift again, eventually.

Maddileh could have coped with no sight; she could have coped with losing her hearing. She might even have coped with losing both—if she knew it would eventually come to an end. But as she sat there in the senseless darkness, she began to think that this might never end, or that some ghost or other creature might kill her before it did end. The only thing that felt real was the hand in hers, and she flexed her fingers occasionally, just to check they were still curled around real, living flesh.

Having her eyes open and seeing nothing began to take its toll on her, so she closed them and concentrated on listening instead. At one point, she shifted, and the sound of sand against cloth was as loud as thunder. Her eyes flew open, and she realised there was a dim blue glow to the world as the light of the orb emerged through the dissolving gloom. Maddileh laughed, a breathy thing that sounded wonderful to her ears. She squeezed Petros's hand, and he squeezed back. "The darkness is leaving," she said, her voice hoarse. "Oh, thank the Allfather, it's going."

A sound partway between a whimper and a groan came from her left where she saw the mage curled up in a foetal position on the floor. Lifting his head, he looked at her and croaked, "Is it over?"

The hand holding Maddileh's fingers squeezed them, then let go. When she turned in that direction, she found she was sitting so close to the bare stone wall of the tunnel that her nose was almost touching it.

FIFTEEN

THE DEMISE AND DEMESNE OF DRAGONS

In the year 699 from the Reckoning, Sir Wenlock, the Knight of the Flowering Moon, set out for the demesne of Hooktooth, who inhabited tunnels in the mountain of Katus. The full story of his quest can be found in the pages preceding this passage, but here we devote space to his squire, Tipp Seyers, a most ingenious boy who provided the Guild with one of its most precious artefacts.

When Sir Wenlock had killed Hooktooth, the dragon immediately began to change state. Squire Seyers told Distinguished Mage Merrick that at first he and his master merely thought that the body was rotting and decomposing at a prodigious rate, but the truth turned out to be much more peculiar and dangerous.

Hooktooth's flesh was, in fact, transmuting into a host of leechlike creatures that slid off the dragon's bones and started in pursuit of the two questers. Readers will note the similarity of this death to that of the Glebe-Reaver, the Vengeful Wyrm, Cadux, and the Emerald Burn, indicating that transmutation of the flesh is a common consequence of a dragon's death. (See Sub-Grand Mage Sorrel's thesis "Legion or Heritage: Flesh Creatures from Earliest Records" for a full discussion of this topic.)

Squire Seyers described to Distinguished Mage Merrick how the creatures looked like leeches but moved like snakes. They also produced a high-pitched screech that, while not overwhelming from a single creature, was apparently quite deafening from such a large host.

The pair of them ran, but Sir Wenlock, being in middle age, was not as swift as his youthful squire. With unrestrained tears, Squire Seyers described to the chroniclers how the knight had told him several times before they went into the lair that Seyers should leave him if his master fell behind. Yet when this very thing happened—when Seyers heard the knight fall and cry out—he turned back with every intention of helping his master. But no sooner had Seyers grasped Sir Wenlock's hand than the leeches were upon them. The old man shrieked as they started to devour him feetfirst where he lay prostrate on the tunnel floor. Amid much sobbing during the retelling, Seyers managed to communicate to us that the knight's final words were, "Tipp, please, I—" before the leeches had swarmed his head and burrowed into his mouth, nose, and ears.

Unable to help his master, Seyers turned and fled back to the outside world, barely able to see for his own tears of grief. It is the opinion of Distinguished Mage Merrick that if not for the leeches pausing to feast upon Sir Wenlock, the squire might not have made it out either. As it was, when he finally lay exhausted on the grass, Seyers became aware of a rustling beside him and found that one of the snake-leeches was chewing through his bag. Terrified but still with great presence of mind, Seyers took up a rock and bashed the creature repeatedly. He described how sparks flew up at the contact and how there was a ringing like steel on stone with every blow (something our investigative mages were able to confirm in their own experiments). Although he failed to kill the creature, Seyers stunned it enough that he was able to shove it into an enchanted flask (one that would fit into a palm but could hold a whole bushel of wheat). The snake-leech was unable to escape such a prison, and Seyers presented it to the Guild when summoned to give his story.

After a barrage of tests, our investigative mages were unable to terminate the creature and so instead created a secure environment for its captivity. At the time of writing, the creature has been observed at all hours and has never once ceased its frenzied movements or attempts to escape.

Seyers received a formal declaration from Sir Wenlock's brother to absolve him of any responsibility in the death of the Knight of the Flowering Moon. Currently, the boy is an apprentice horse-guard at Peverill Castle.

SIXTEEN

Maddileh had expected some warning that they were about to emerge into the dragon's main lair. When she'd gone with Sir Osbert to take down the Shimmering Corsair, the increasingly hot air and sharp scent of molten metal had alerted her to their proximity. But she and Petros simply walked down a sloping tunnel at the bottom of which they found themselves in the open cavern of the White Lady's main lair. The orb of direction flickered, went out, then fell to the floor with a soft thud.

"I . . . Oh my . . ." Petros murmured, his eyes wide. Even Maddileh, who had seen a cave full of treasure before, was taken aback by the wealth on display. "There's so much of it," the mage whispered.

"The White Lady has been around a long time," Maddileh said, her eyes scanning the treasure heaps and rock ledges for any sign of the dragon. Light came from flames feeding on little piles of a sticky black substance. Some hunters called it *bile fire* because it was something a dragon excreted from its insides, like a hair ball vomited up by a cat. But its exact nature had never been determined because no container could hold it long enough to allow examination.

"Don't walk too close to the flames," Maddileh instructed. "If your cloak catches fire from that stuff, you'll never put it out."

"Look at the size of that silver plate!" Petros said excitedly. "And I can see a crown, and a . . . a . . ." He frowned. "Is that a tin roof?"

"Probably sparkled invitingly in the moonlight. Now, come on and help me."

Together, they searched the cave, looking for both Petros's sister and the sword but finding neither. They saw no dragon either, which worried Maddileh no end. They moved quietly, peering into the many small offshoots and alcoves that dotted the edges of the cave. After an hour, they'd barely covered even a quarter of it, and they decided to split up to cover more ground but not to go too far in case of danger.

"May you walk the Bridge untroubled," Maddileh said before they parted.

Petros rolled his eyes. "I have no plans to die down here."

A pile of ash and molten metal caught Maddileh's eye, and she knelt to examine it. She knew incinerated human remains when she saw them; the ash had an oily, clumping quality that you'd never find in the ashes of an ordinary fire. The sight brought dream memories thundering into her mind, and she got dizzy at the idea of what it must be like to be caught in dragon fire. Putting out a hand to steady herself, she accidentally knocked the top off the pile of ash, getting some on her fingers. Disgusted, she wiped them on the side of her trousers, her stomach churning with the violation and a premonition of bad luck settling on her. Then she saw something glinting within the pile of ash. Bracing herself against the revulsion, she pulled the object out and cleaned it off. It was a ring, burned and twisted by intense heat, the onyx in the centre cracked and grey, but still recognisable: it was the twin of the one Kennion had given her.

Curious, she extended her hand to compare the two and realised her own ring was missing. She cast around, looking for it, even though it had been most likely lost in the tunnels somewhere. With a shudder, she thought of the unknown hand she'd held in the darkness; as it retreated, had it slipped the ring from her numb fingers? And what did it mean that she'd found its twin down here in a pile of dead knight?

The sense of dreadful surrealism was heightened when a voice she knew but had never expected to hear in this place said, "I will *not* give it to you. Any trust I had in you is now firmly shattered."

Slipping the unsettling ring into her pocket as a mystery for later, Maddileh stood up to face the two people coming towards her: Petros and his sister, Saralene. The two of them were arguing in low, heated voices, and Saralene was only five steps away from Maddileh when she noticed the knight. She stopped dead, her eyes widening.

"What are you doing here?"

Hoping her own shock didn't show on her face, Maddileh gestured to her armour. "Hunting dragons. You?"

Saralene opened her mouth to reply, then narrowed her eyes at her brother and muttered, "It's a long story."

During this brief exchange, Petros's gaze had been flicking between the two women. Although his surprise and curiosity were written plain on his face, he clearly decided it could wait, and he said, "We should really be going. Take that damn thing off, will you, Saralene? I told you that's what drew the dragon to you."

"Yes, you did," Saralene said coldly, "but I already worked that out for myself. What would be more helpful is if you could tell me why you gave me an enchanted amulet in the first place."

Petros rolled his eyes, giving Maddileh an exasperated look, but the knight only had half her attention on the conversation; a movement on the rock shelf above them had caught her eye. She peered upwards into the shadows of the roof.

"It was a mistake," Petros said. "I'm sorry—an honest mistake. I didn't know, and when I realised what had happened, I came as quickly as I could."

"As quickly as that time you raced to fetch help when I was drowning in the lake?"

The White Lady was an old dragon, a clever dragon. By all accounts, her scales shone a brilliant white in daylight, but what colour would she be in her own home? In the gloom of her lair?

"That was a long time ago and totally different."

Few knights had survived an encounter with the White Lady; those who did return spoke of how she materialised out of nowhere.

"Not that different, when you think about it."

"I told you I was running to help then, and I'm telling you I came to help now. Why won't you believe me?"

Maybe her scales were like water and reflected her surroundings. Sunlight would appear dazzling in a lake, but a cavern pool would also take on the colour of the stones around it.

From the ledge above, a large grey wing stretched out.

"I'm sorry I ever came after you, Saralene. Stay here and starve or rot in a dragon's belly for all I care."

Never taking her eyes off the dragon, Maddileh put out a hand to stop Petros walking past her. "Squire," she said softly as a great serpentine head leaned over the edge; golden eyes peered down at them. "I want you to give me my spear and then run."

Both Petros and Saralene looked up. In the next instant, Petros shoved the spear at Maddileh and then was pelting back the way they'd come. The dragon glanced lazily towards him before returning her attention to the two women below her. Maddileh gazed up into eyes that had seen centuries; she glimpsed a flash of teeth that had devoured countless victims. Firelight danced along the creature's scales, making her hide appear crusted with jewels.

For the first time in her life, Maddileh was scared enough to run away. She had never been scared in the tourney. She might have been afraid when she ventured into the Silken Sigh's demesne, but that fear had not prevented her putting one foot in front of the other. She'd been petrified to see her master battle the Shimmering Corsair, but she'd stood her ground and answered his call for help. And although she'd been terrified, standing on those stairs in just her nightgown, her brothers cowering behind her as a trio of grinning reavers advanced up the stairs, she wouldn't have run then for all the gold in the fourteen realms.

But now all she wanted to do was flee those ageless eyes, those sharp teeth, and those talons that could disembowel her with one flick. The White Lady was old. The White Lady was cunning. The White Lady was looking right at her.

Something landed at her feet, breaking the dreadful mesmer of the dragon, and Maddileh glanced down to see the emerald necklace that Saralene had been wearing.

"It's enchanted," Saralene said. "I haven't been able to leave while I was wearing it. She follows it wherever it goes. If I leave it here, that might be enough to distract her while we run."

"I'm game to give it a go," Maddileh replied. Slowly, the two of them started walking backward. The White Lady didn't move, but neither did her eyes leave them. She didn't even glance at the discarded necklace. When the two women were halfway across the cavern, Maddileh allowed herself a small flicker of hope that they might make it. Then the White Lady shifted and jumped down from the ledge with the grace of a cat.

The dragon didn't rush them; she walked with a lazy sway to her body, but the length of her stride meant she quickly halved the distance. "Run!" Maddileh said, turning to find that Saralene was already doing so.

They were almost at the mouth of one of the tunnels when a great clawed hand swept Saralene off her feet and sent her flying. Momentum kept Maddileh going for a few more paces, and part of her wanted to keep running, to flee back to the safety of the sunlight. But another part of her knew she couldn't live with the guilt of leaving Saralene behind. She was no Sir Warbrick. Turning back, she drew her sword and faced the dragon, who had also halted and was staring at her.

I cannot die. I will not die.

The words seemed small and weak in her head.

From the corner of her eye, Maddileh saw Saralene staggering to her feet; that was good, but she needed to lead the White Lady away if Saralene was to have any hope of escaping. Just as she was racing through possible options in her mind, the dragon brought its head down close and looked at Maddileh. A voice echoed in the knight's head.

What kind of creature are you, little dirt-walker?

Maddileh staggered back as if caught by a physical blow. This close, she would have seen the dragon's lips if they'd moved; they hadn't. But she'd heard the White Lady speak with a voice like a rich, aged wine.

The White Lady tilted her head slightly. *Clearly, a creature that can hear me. How novel.*

"I'm a knight," Maddileh said, taking a step forward. Her voice barely shook.

You are certainly dressed as one, the White Lady conceded, *but you look . . . peculiar.*

During this exchange, Maddileh had taken slow steps to the left, away from Saralene. Now, she had a clear run towards the distant reaches of the cave. Her best plan was to dodge among the stalactites and piles of treasure, always keeping something between her and the dragon as she did a circuit and hopefully arrived back at the exit.

Looking up at the White Lady, Maddileh said, "I am the Knight of the Stairs, and I've come for the Fireborne Blade."

Her words wrought an immediate change on the White Lady. The dragon visibly tensed and her eyes narrowed. She had looked dangerous before; now she looked lethal.

I cannot let you take that man-fang, she said, the voice soft and threatening.

"I didn't think you would," Maddileh said, and an instant later, she was pelting across the ground. The White Lady roared, and Maddileh sensed something coming at her very fast. She dived for the floor, her armour shrieking as she slid along the smooth stone. Above her, the White Lady's massive tail split the air so hard and fast that there was a whipcrack of thunder.

Scrambling to her feet again, Maddileh raced towards a pile of gold. Dragons were large, powerful beasts, capable of wreaking great destruction. But they could be slow.

Maddileh remembered Sir Alfonso offering her advice before they set out: "A black kite might be a large bird with powerful talons that can kill a falcon in a single strike. But a falcon is small and swift, and if it is also smart, if it dodges and dives, it will escape the kite every time."

So Maddileh became a falcon, slipping through crevices, curling around corners, always staying just out of reach from hooked talons and snapping jaws.

She can talk. She can talk, Maddileh thought as she dashed here and there. Despite the terrible danger, she felt a deep sense of awe at such a discovery. She'd read all the volumes of *The Demise and Demesne of Dragons* that her aunt had owned, and during tourneys, she had spoken to knights who'd hunted dragons and wyrms, but none of them had ever heard a dragon talk. *Think what the mages will say when I tell them about this. If I survive to tell them, of course.*

No. I cannot die. I will not die. Not here. Not now.

She ran, clutching her spear and sword, praying she wouldn't have to use them, thinking only of escaping. And then she saw it: the Fireborne Blade. She'd passed various swords and armour as she strived to escape, but none of them had looked like this. It lacked a cross guard—this was a blade for a single killing blow, not a fight. The pommel was circular with a dragon on it, and the blade had a moving shimmer to it, like ripples on water. It seemed to glow with some internal light. The sight of it halted her in her tracks, and she stood staring.

I could do it, I could really do it. I could take it and—

The White Lady turned a corner; the dragon stopped,

her golden eyes flicking between Maddileh and the sword. Slowly, as if laying down a weapon, she tucked her wings into her sides, diminishing her size but not the sense of threat she exuded.

Please, metal-wearer, pick some other treasure. I cannot let you take that.

Maddileh looked at the sword resting against the wall, untarnished by age or use. Saralene was forgotten; her own life was insignificant. Only the Blade mattered. Planting her feet solidly on the ground, bending herself slightly for any onslaught, she replied softly, "I didn't think you would."

Maddileh had expected the dragon to lunge at her, but the White Lady didn't move. She stayed still, alert, and Maddileh wondered if the dragon was weighing her options. But then she saw that while the head and neck were immobile, the creature's sides were pumping faster and faster. *Like bellows,* Maddileh thought a split second before the White Lady opened her mouth and a stream of white-hot flame roared towards her.

There was no time to duck or dive aside, so Maddileh merely bowed her head and braced herself for the impact, her heart stuttering in her chest.

I cannot die. I will not—

The heat was searing, agonising, scouring her down to her bones. It was her nightmare made real.

Then it was over, and Maddileh was still whole. She raised her head and looked at the molten metal around her that hissed and ticked as it cooled. She looked down at her body: the unmarked armour, her clothes not even singed.

Her spear was still whole, although her sword was now a steel puddle on the floor. Laughter bubbled up out of her, and the White Lady gaped, her massive dragon jaws parted in shock.

"I survived!" Maddileh cried. The White Lady roared, and then another bout of fire came at Maddileh. She endured the agony with a grim smile of triumph on her face.

I cannot die. I will not die.

As the last of the flames died away, Maddileh snatched up the Fireborne Blade, then charged forward with a battle cry. The White Lady backed away, her eyes darting nervously here and there. *What is this? This cannot be. What manner of thing are you?*

Maddileh wasted no breath on a reply but hacked at her enemy's feet and legs, the only parts of a dragon covered by leathery skin rather than scales. A sword could pierce that, although such a hit would likely only enrage the dragon rather than causing it any lasting damage. But enraging the White Lady, drawing her head closer to her prey, was exactly what Maddileh wanted. During her many centuries, the White Lady had never suffered a missing scale or developed a weak spot. There was only one place that a spear could be driven into her flesh, and few knights would have the bravery to try.

Swinging her sword at an upraised foot, Maddileh managed to slice through the softer skin. The White Lady bellowed in pain and lifted her foot away. With no sheath for the Blade, Maddileh dropped the weapon on the floor, her fingers aching at its loss the second she let go, and gripped her spear with both hands. After twisting the two sections of the engraved central band in opposite directions, she readied herself.

Eyes filled with fury and pain, the White Lady lunged at Maddileh, opening her jaws wide to bite the knight in two. Maddileh bent her knees and then launched herself upwards into that terrifying maw. As she jabbed the spear into the dragon's gums, her eyes were drawn towards the creature's throat where fire bubbled and burned.

The White Lady shook her head, her tongue writhing so violently that Maddileh lost her balance and tumbled to the floor with a jarring thud. Instantly, she rolled to avoid being crushed beneath the dragon's descending foot. Bellowing, the White Lady shook her head and clawed at her mouth, trying to wrench the spear free, but its barbed tip held it fast, and her large claws were not dexterous enough to pry it loose. Maddileh watched as the poison from the spear took hold, causing the White Lady to sway, her eyes to become unfocused. As she watched the dragon stagger sluggishly and then slump to the floor, Maddileh was surprised to find grief rising within her. There was no triumph in seeing those intelligent golden eyes lose their lustre nor any pleasure in witnessing this graceful creature become as clumsy as a drunk.

The dragon lay on the floor, her legs now limp and useless; the only movement was her chest rising and falling with her rapid, panicked breathing.

Maddileh walked over as the White Lady tried to lift her front leg in one final effort to dislodge the spear. There was a new sparkle to the dragon as frost began to form along her body. Kneeling down by the creature's head, Maddileh whispered, "I'm sorry."

The eyes rolled in their sockets, the pupils dilated. *Where did you . . . get that . . . spear? What . . . are . . . you?*

Frost whitened the dragon's eyeballs, and the White Lady finally lay still. Feeling a tightness on her cheeks, Maddileh reached up to her face and pulled away a bead of ice, a frozen tear she'd wept without knowing.

The frost was starting to spread across the floor now, and Maddileh backed away, her breath misting before her face.

"Goodbye, my lady," she whispered before retrieving the Fireborne Blade and hurrying after her companions.

SEVENTEEN

THREE MONTHS AGO

Maddileh sat relishing the last warmth in the autumn sun and considered the spear in her hands.

A blow to the mouth or gums, the eye, or the inner ear were going to be the most efficacious, as the poison would then go straight to the White Lady's brain. Her aunt—guardian of the Weldrake Repository—had instructed her to twist the metal bands in the middle before using it. "To activate the poison, I think," her aunt had said, "although I'm not sure how it works exactly. It's so old."

Sitting outside the inn, Maddileh let her gaze wander to the trees bedecked with orange and red leaves. *It's going to be a hard winter,* she thought. *Little Marcus hates the winter. He always gets too cold. I can't earn tourney money or prizes anymore, but I could go home and help in other ways—train Father's guards, care for the horses, chop wood even.* Her gaze returned to the spear. If she went home, she'd be a ghost, drifting aimlessly and uselessly. The letter in her jacket crinkled as she picked up her drink and drained it. Before her was not a choice of death or glory, it was a question of which life she wanted: the one she'd felt was right in her bones from the moment she picked up a sword, or the one someone else crafted for her.

"Sir Maddileh?" She looked up to see a tall man with soft brown hair and a charming smile that did not reach his calculating eyes.

"Yes."

"I am Petros." The young man held out his hand; Maddileh didn't take it or even look at it. Petros withdrew his hand, his expression getting several degrees chillier. "May I sit down?" She gestured to a chair. "I can see that you're a busy woman, and I don't want to detain you. In fact, I want to accompany you."

"Oh?"

"Yes, I'm a mage and—"

"I don't take mages anywhere." From the look he gave her, she might as well have slapped him. He tried to recover his smile.

"Yes, but I hoped—"

Maddileh stood up. "Mages are a liability in dragon lairs. All that magic messes with their heads. I've seen the scars on knights that prove that. Nothing you can say can convince me to take you with me."

"But—"

"Nothing." Gripping the spear tightly, she started to walk away, but the man sprang up in front of her.

"There is something in that cave that I desperately need. I *am* going to go with you, but it can be the easy way or the hard way."

"Doesn't matter, they're both my way, and I'm not taking you," she said and strode off, squinting against the glare of the setting sun.

EIGHTEEN

Maddileh stared at the Fireborne Blade. It filled her thoughts, and even though she constantly yearned to touch it, she loathed it too. All she could think of was that the way it flashed in the light reminded her of dragon scales.

She died to keep it hidden.

She could talk, she wasn't just a beast.

And I killed her.

Saralene sat with her back against the wall, a mutinous expression on her face. She and Petros had been icily silent ever since they'd left the lair several hours ago. Maddileh couldn't fathom why Saralene was cross with her brother for rescuing her, but both of them looked ready to tear into someone at the slightest provocation, so she kept her curiosity to herself and stayed out of the way.

Petros was pouring duplication potion onto some bread and dried beef slices. "You're doing it wrong," Saralene said tartly.

"It's duplicating potion. You *can't* do it wrong."

"And yet you are. Here, let—"

"No!" Petros held the bottle out of reach as Saralene went to take it. Maddileh felt as if she were back in the nursery.

"Fine. I'll pour the water. That way at least I'll be able

to stomach something of this meal." Saralene retrieved the water flask and cups from one of the bags.

They ate and drank in silence; all the food was tasteless mush, but the water was fresh and cold. They'd been able to fill their flasks from a fast-flowing stream they'd come across during their trek. Now the dragon was dead, they could walk out through the main entrance normally utilised by the White Lady. Maddileh had thought it would be a direct tunnel up and out, but while this passage was wider, it twisted and turned just as much as any of the others.

The sound of a cup falling to the floor drew her gaze to Petros, who seemed to have finished his meal and fallen into an exhausted sleep. Saralene put a finger to her lips; Maddileh frowned. After a few more moments, Saralene reached over and poked her brother hard. He snorted but didn't wake.

"I think he's out," Saralene said. "He should be like that for several hours now, but we'll still have to work fast."

"What? I don't understand."

Saralene sat down in front of Maddileh, her sullenness replaced by an urgent energy that brightened her smoky eyes. "Didn't you wonder why I was in the cave?"

"Well, yes, obviously. But you didn't seem in a talkative mood, so I didn't like to ask."

"A few weeks ago, my brother turned up at my door with a gift—an emerald necklace. There are . . . complications in our family, branches that don't speak to one another, that kind of thing. He told me that the necklace was an heirloom he'd recovered that had once belonged to our mother. He said he couldn't keep it but didn't want anyone else in the family to possess it, so he supposed that I should have it."

"That was . . . generous?" Maddileh hazarded.

"Suspicious is what it was. The last thing my brother ever gave me was a slap when I accidentally spilt some wine over his precious magic books. But when he turned up with the necklace, I pretended to be what he thought me to be: a vain, grasping female who was only too happy to have a beautiful necklace of my own. I figured if he wanted me to have it, then it must benefit him in some way, and I wanted to find out how.

"So, Kennion and I studied it for almost a week and discovered an enchantment set in one of the flaws in the setting. It's very high-level magic, quite beyond my brother's skills, so he must have had help. It was an enchantment to summon a dragon."

"But why did he want the dragon to take you? If he was annoyed at you using magic, surely there are better ways to get rid of you—no offence meant."

"Magic has always run in our family. I have some latent power. That's why I went to work for Kennion—he was helping me to draw it out. If I can activate it, I could become a mage, a powerful one too, Kennion reckons. But if I can't and it remains hidden, it's most likely that any sons I have will inherit it.

"Now, practice, concentration, and knowledge can help bring out latent talent, but there is one way that will ensure it blossoms: by exposing the individual to an incredibly strong source of magic."

"Like being stuck in a cave with a dragon, for example," Maddileh said, "and then exposed to all the magic at their death." Grief twisted her guts at the thought of the lifeless dragon below, of beauty dulled. "But your brother doesn't seem like the sort who would appreciate a powerful mage as a sister, so what's in it for him?"

Saralene bit her lip. "I think he is going to try to drain my newfound magic and find some way to give it to the High Mage."

"The High Mage? Why—" Maddileh paused as Petros snorted and shifted in his sleep. Then she went on in a quieter voice, "Why doesn't he keep it for himself?"

With a wry smile, Saralene said, "Oh, my brother may think he's the best of our family, but he's really an idiot, although he's smart enough to realise he's an idiot, if that makes sense." She ran her hands through her hair, suddenly looking weary. "There's a lot of backstory that would take too long, but let's just say that if he took all my magic, he wouldn't be clever enough to keep it for himself, and someone else would likely just take it off him in a similar manner. But if he gives it to the High Mage and prolongs the old man's life, then he earns the gratitude of the second-most powerful man in the fourteen realms, and that will protect him against anything."

"Then let's go," Maddileh said, starting to stand up. "Let's leave him here and—"

"No," said Saralene, gripping her arm surprisingly tightly and pulling her down. "If we leave him, he'll just come after me at a later date. Or if not him," she added, sensing that Maddileh was about to protest that he couldn't come after her if he couldn't find his way out of the caves, "someone else will—someone that I *can't* stop."

"So you *can* stop him? How?"

She bit her lip again, and the sight caused Maddileh's heart to stutter. "I'm sorry, but because you saved me in the cave, I can't tell you what I'm planning."

"What? That makes no sense."

Saralene gave a little laugh. "Welcome to the world of magic." She pulled over one of Petros's bags and dug around in it before pulling out the green bowl. With a sigh, she muttered, "I guessed right, then."

Maddileh was itching to ask just what she'd guessed, but she knew Saralene wouldn't tell her until she was good and ready. *Damn these arrogant mages.*

Saralene looked up and said, "There's one last thing that I need to tell you. I could have sent you to sleep too, kept this a secret, but I . . ." She hesitated, looking as if she was swallowing words that were on the tip of her tongue. "Look, my brother is using you as much as he's using me, and if you help me now and trust me, I can save us both."

"Don't be ridiculous. He's not using me. I wouldn't let him. I'd have a sword in his guts before he could try."

"You don't need to trust me absolutely. You just need to trust me more than you trust him." Saralene pointed at the sleeping figure. "If I say he's already cast a spell on you, would you trust me enough to let me try to help you break free of it?"

Maddileh narrowed her eyes. "What kind of spell?"

"If I tell you, it will unravel."

"Good."

"And then so will you."

"Oh." Maddileh thought for some time, weighing up all the strange things that had happened on this trip, wondering when Petros had found the time to cast a spell on her. When they walked to the caves, maybe? Her memory of that was hazy. Perhaps when she was sitting in the dark, thinking she was holding his hand? Maybe when she was sleeping. In the end, did it matter when? The question was: Did she believe Saralene, and did she trust her?

"I trust you," Maddileh said softly, feeling her cheeks redden.

Saralene beamed. "Wonderful. Then hold this." She pushed the bowl into Maddileh's hands before standing up and tugging her skirts up to reveal smooth, pale thighs. Embarrassed, Maddileh looked away, but not before she saw a small pouch tied around Saralene's middle by a length of ribbon. When Saralene sat back down again, she was holding a knife, some thin red ribbon, and two feathers that glimmered as if they were made of gold.

"What are those?" Maddileh asked, entranced by their shimmer.

"Phoenix feathers," Saralene replied as she used her knife to cut a strand of her hair, which she then began to plait with the ribbon. "Kennion and I not only managed to discover what Petros had in mind, we also managed to find a way to set me up so that I could foil his plans once he came for me." She was grinning, her eyes sparkling with her own cleverness.

When the braid was complete, she used the knife to cut her leg, then smeared the braid with her blood. Once one side of it was sticky, she wrapped the braid around the feather, and the blood stuck the two together. "All right, your turn," Saralene said. She sliced a strand of Maddileh's hair and plaited it the same way. "Leg or arm?" she asked, picking up the knife. "It doesn't matter which so long as we can cover it up again. If Petros wakes to find cuts on us, he'll be suspicious."

"Arm," Maddileh said, rolling up her sleeve. The thought of exposing her legs and having Saralene touch them set a heavy ball in the bottom of her stomach.

Saralene made the cut then started to apply the blood to the braid. But when she held it up, the blood had turned to dark sand that slid off. "Why is my blood doing that?" Maddileh asked, alarmed.

"It happens sometimes," Saralene said, not meeting her eyes.

"This is about the spell Petros has cast on me, isn't it?"

"Hush, I need to think," Saralene said, frowning as she stared at the braid.

With great effort and huge reluctance, Maddileh reined in her other questions and let the mage think.

"All done," Saralene said eventually, "I think if we combine our blood, then the spell should still work. It's not ideal, and it might have unforeseen consequences, but it's better than the alternative." Scraping the lump of congealed blood off her leg, Saralene dipped the braid in her own blood before smearing more of Maddileh's blood onto it. This time, the braid and feather stuck together. Saralene let out a shaky breath and smiled. "Excellent." She placed the two feathers in the bowl and poured water on them until they were submerged. Maddileh noted that the phoenix feathers didn't float to the surface like other feathers would but instead sat on the bottom of the bowl like stones.

"You said that mixing our blood was better than the alternative," Maddileh said. "If I asked you what the alternative was, would you tell me?" Saralene looked at her, her smile apologetic but her eyes steely. "Fine. Then do you need me to do anything to help?"

"No. I need to enchant the water to create a false bottom to the bowl, hiding the feathers. The enchantment of the bowl itself will disguise the magic of the feathers, a bit like the sun outshines a candle." She grinned. "Petros won't know they're there until it's too late. The best thing you can do is settle down and rest. Make sure you pretend to be sound asleep when Petros wakes up. He'll be groggy from the drug, but he won't get suspicious if we appear groggy too."

"All right," Maddileh said, stretching out on the tunnel floor. She lay with her eyes open, watching Saralene while she looked down into the bowl, chanting. After a while, the bowl began to glow, and the reflection of light on water rippled over Saralene's face and danced over the cold tunnel walls. The mage's words were soft, almost musical, and they soothed Maddileh into sleep, the brightness of the bowl lighting the inside of her eyelids with brilliant colours.

NINETEEN

Maddileh was awakened by the sound of groans and shuffling. Instinctively, she opened her eyes and saw Petros elbowing himself up. Saralene's warning floated across her mind, and Maddileh instantly shut her eyes, concentrating on keeping her breathing gentle and regular. There was silence for a while, and Maddileh imagined Petros staring at his companions, suspicion wriggling like a sick worm through his mind. Then she heard the sound of him searching through his bag.

On the other side of the tunnel, Saralene shifted and muttered, "What time is it?"

"Time you slatterns were awake," Petros said coldly.

Maddileh went rigid, her nails digging into her palms at the insult. Belatedly, she realised that if Petros was watching her, he'd have noticed her tense, so if she continued to feign sleep, he'd know something was up. So she opened one eye. When she saw him staring right at her, she asked, "What was that you said, squire?"

He stiffened, then said sullenly, "I am not your squire. I thought you understood that."

Maddileh raised herself up, keeping her movements slow

and sluggish. "If that's the case, then why do you continue to carry the bags?"

Petros's hand tightened around the strap. Saralene smirked.

"She's got you there, brother. Perhaps we should take turns in carrying the supplies—unless your supplies include something you stole from the White Lady's hoard?"

His face carefully neutral, Petros picked up a satchel and tossed it to Saralene. "The only treasure I liberated from that lair was you, sweet sister," he said, his voice dripping with sarcasm, "and now I'm wondering why I bothered. Carry the damn thing if you want, but don't complain to me if your shoulders ache."

As he packed his sleeping blanket away, Maddileh and Saralene shared a look; he'd not thrown the bag containing the bowl to her. He'd kept that one close.

Once they set out again, it became clear that Saralene hadn't been faking her grogginess upon waking—she was genuinely exhausted. Her feet scuffed the sand with every step, and her shoulders slumped lower and lower.

Petros, who was in the lead, kept turning round and scowling at his sister until he eventually snapped, "What is the matter with you? You're slowing us down." He moved as if to grab her, but Maddileh stepped forward and took Saralene's arm first. The mage's skin was delightfully soft but unpleasantly clammy.

"It's the magic," Maddileh said, staring down Petros. "I've seen it before. When a dragon dies and all its magic is released, it can overwhelm anyone nearby, especially if there's magic in their blood, which I guess there is given she's your sister. Magic fatigue, I think they call it." Petros glared at her. Maddileh, who was making this up as she went, asked, "Don't *you* feel sluggish too?"

He narrowed his eyes. "I've never heard of magic fatigue, and my knowledge of magic is extensive."

Maddileh shrugged. "You get your knowledge from books, I get mine from living experiences firsthand. What can I say? There are some things you can't learn from reading."

The three of them stood there: Petros glaring, Maddileh carefully casual, and Saralene's gaze flicking between them.

Giving his sister one final glare, Petros said, "Pull yourself together or we'll never get out of here." Then he turned on his heel and stormed ahead.

Despite Petros's huffs of disgust and sly backward glances, it wasn't long before they reached the tunnel entrance. There had been no hint it was approaching, no gradual lightening of the gloom; they just followed a curve in the tunnel, and suddenly, a jagged circle of light was ahead.

Maddileh laughed with pure joy and started forward, but Petros held out a hand to block her way. "We must be careful. There may be danger ahead."

"I'm pretty sure the danger is behind us," Maddileh said impatiently.

"A doorway is always a magical place, doubly so if it's associated with dragons. It's a boundary, a meeting of two worlds. Malign influences might have been drawn to it. Let me examine the way first."

Maddileh glanced at Saralene who shrugged, then nodded.

The adept's face was grey and unhealthy, making Maddileh wonder if there was something beyond exhaustion troubling her.

Petros approached the entrance and began to remove items from his bag that he held near the entrance: a twig, a dagger, a crystal on a cord. He ran his fingers over the air, muttering. Then he turned to them, beaming. "It's safe! We can leave. It's all over. Help my sister, would you, knight, while I pack away my things."

Maddileh helped Saralene forward, the other woman's hand gripping her own so tightly that Maddileh's full attention was on Saralene, meaning she didn't see Petros whirl around until it was too late. The dagger in his hand sliced open Saralene's throat, and as his sister staggered, Petros thrust the jade bowl underneath her so it would catch her gushing blood.

With a furious cry, Maddileh went for her sword, but Petros spoke a strange, guttural word, and Maddileh found herself pinned back against the tunnel wall. The Fireborne Blade, jolted free from her grasp by the impact, lay useless and frustratingly out of reach on the floor. Maddileh couldn't move—couldn't even breathe—and could only watch as Saralene sank to her knees, her grey skin turning a bloodless white. Petros gripped Saralene's shoulders, supporting her and angling her over the bowl until the flow of blood lessened to a dribble, to a drip, to nothing. Then he cast her body aside with a look of disgust, placed the lid on the bowl, and wiped his bloody hands on her clothes.

Maddileh might have been as immobile as a statue, but she was a frenzy of fury and grief on the inside as Petros walked towards her.

With a sneer twisting his features, he said, "No living man can defeat the White Lady. No. Living. Man. And you, in your arrogance, thought the loophole was that you were a woman!" He gave a snort of laughter. "But you missed the truth. It was *I* who figured it out. No *living* man can kill the White Lady. No one alive could defeat her. Look out there, *knight*," he said with disdain, pointing to the outside world, which held blue skies and blossom. A dragonfly zipped past, its scales flashing blue. "You entered the caves in autumn—don't you remember? And now it's spring."

I did come here in autumn, yes. I remember walking up the hillside with the leaves swirling around me. And then I remember standing in the entrance, looking at the blossom falling. But it can't be . . . I only just came in, didn't I?

"It's a trick," she said, her throat and jaw working hard against whatever enchantment bound her.

He gave an amused chuckle.

"That's right. It is a trick, but not the kind you think. You died down here, knight, many months ago. I had to perform quite a complex spell to summon your bones, armour, and spear up to the entrance. It would have been so much easier if I could have been there when you died, but I couldn't convince you to take me. Still, my skill in magic meant that didn't matter too much. Then, just a lock of your hair, some magic, and there you were, standing in the entrance again, looking dazed and believing everything I told you." His fingers plucked at the unknown bracelet on her wrist. "Of course, the dragon fire burned up everything but your bones. There should have been no hair left to make a charm braid, but luckily, Sir Allerbon was in possession of some, and he was happy to give it up. I didn't even need to bribe him very much; he was pleased to be rid of it."

Maddileh's muscles screamed in protest, desperate to kick out at him, to lock her fingers around his throat and squeeze. His eyes held no fear, only amusement at this final betrayal. He glanced over his shoulder.

"If you want to hear all the truths, of course, then I should add that my sister killed you. She didn't mean to, of course. That ring Kennion gave you—it cancels out enchantments, doesn't it? Enchantments like, say, magic armour . . ."

"No!" Her voice was croaky, even that single syllable an immense effort.

Petros shrugged. "That part is just guesswork. He might have intended such a consequence, he might not. He's a respected mage, but his mind's going, if you ask me, so it might have been a mistake. Perhaps it was the armour itself. Perhaps the blacksmith was lying when he said it would protect you. I can think of at least a dozen ways to convince a stupid knight that armour was dragon-proof."

Maddileh thought of the powder the blacksmith had thrown on the flames—had that been a trick? But the stones had melted . . . Had Kennion tricked her, then? Her gut said no, but he was the one who gave her the name of the armourer, and it was he who gave her the ring also. But he couldn't be in on Petros's plot, could he? Not if he was helping Saralene. But maybe she was just another pawn too.

"Whatever the cause of your death, it has certainly been useful," Petros continued. "After I realised the chink in the prophecy, it was the High Mage who put forward your name as an ideal candidate. We needed a dead knight made corporeal again to kill the White Lady, to release a huge blast of magic to activate my sister's latent power, but crucially, that knight must not think of themselves as a ghost. The High Mage had heard of your stubbornness, your determination not to be beaten or cowed—and, of course, your desperation to prove yourself. We could give your soul a new body in the confident knowledge that your mind would accept you were still alive." He cocked his head, false sympathy on his face. "Those nightmares of yours, about dying in flames—did you think they were the sole product of your mind? Or the touch of a ghost? Poor Maddileh, you were reliving your own death night after night."

No. No. No!

"But now you've served your purpose, and I can let you rest for eternity while I enjoy the spoils of our trip." He retrieved his dagger from the floor; it was still covered with Saralene's blood. He slid the tip under the bracelet. "Blood and bones and hair and belief—all a ghost needs to make it live again. Temporarily at least. It's the basis of all life, you know. What am I saying? Of course you don't know. Your knowledge comes from experience, not from books," he added with a sly smile.

Maddileh could feel his hands around her arm, but she couldn't force her body to do anything. Her mind raged at her body's stupidity, its faithless compliance, and still she couldn't move.

"But the Allmother and Allfather forged us from dirt, and to dirt we must all return. Goodbye, Maddileh. It has been useful knowing you."

The blade snicked through the bracelet, and Maddileh's skin became brown and grainy. Her flesh turned to soil and sand, sliding off her bones. It didn't hurt—in fact, she didn't feel anything; her body was numb and it was only her soul that raged. She watched her body disintegrating, her mind screaming defiance to the last.

"Perhaps my sister's ghost will keep you company," Petros said, "and perhaps the High Mage will give me a pretty price for this sword of yours." His voice was a final, distant sound before silence surged swiftly around her.

TWENTY

Maddileh stared at the tree before her, its blossom shed but its leaves so green it hurt her eyes. Yet she welcomed the discomfort—nothing else hurt, and it should do. She should feel betrayed, violated, vengeful, devastated. Petros had used her and then discarded her; he had even taken the Fireborne Blade.

"Maddileh?"

She shouldn't exist. The White Lady's death should have sucked all the magic from the caves. Maddileh should be reducing by degrees, dwindling to nothing. Was it something in Petros's spell that kept her tied here? Would she never pass on but stay here, looking forever at a lost world?

"Maddileh? You need to look at me."

Maddileh squeezed her eyes shut, locking herself away from the painfully bright world. What was the use of existing if she couldn't feel the—

"Maddileh. *Look* at me."

—breeze on her skin, the scents of summer or the cold of winter. But how much worse would it be if she *could* smell and taste a world she was no longer a part of?

A hand gripped her shoulder, making her jump and open her eyes. Saralene crouched next to her, impossibly whole and beautiful. Maddileh's eyes drifted down the tunnel to the adept's decaying body. The paradox nearly sent her mind spiraling into the waiting abyss. But if Saralene was here, there were things to be said. Who knew how long the White Lady's magic would keep them as ghosts.

"I'm sorry I couldn't save you," Maddileh murmured, and for the first time since Petros's departure, she felt a spark of emotion: it was a sickening, guilty grief, but it was so much better than the void she'd been inhabiting.

"Dying was certainly not the best outcome, but it seemed the only logical step to achieve my goal."

Maddileh gaped, first with confusion, then with suspicion. Many of the mages she'd encountered had shown a marked disinterest in the lives and deaths of others, but they valued their own skin highly. "You don't care that he killed you?" The spark was dwindling within her, the weary numbness returning.

In contrast, Saralene's eyes blazed.

"Of course I care," she snarled. "That odious pig has hated me since the day I was born. The thought that he's out there, gloating, makes me sick as anything." She'd clenched her fists, but now she uncurled them, evidently fighting back her anger. But her fury was like a flame, drawing Maddileh in; Saralene's rage stirred up her own feelings.

And as the ability to feel and care reawakened within her, Maddileh felt an urgent, bitter question rising up her throat.

"Did you know?"

"I suspected that Petros would—"

"Did you know that Kennion's ring would cancel out the enchantment on the armour? That I'd march into the White Lady's lair unprotected?"

Saralene stared at her, and Maddileh couldn't tell if her shocked expression was genuine or carefully crafted to cover her guilt.

"Kennion told me where to go for the armour *and* he gave me the ring. Was that all part of your plan to foil Petros?"

Saralene looked down, picking at a nail. "That was never part of the plan that I knew about."

"That's no answer at all."

"Please, Maddileh—I didn't know, I swear. I don't believe that Kennion realised it either. He's a good man."

"He's a mage."

"And a good man," Saralene insisted. "He meant that gift generously, I'm sure of it. And if I had realised what would happen, I swear I would have taken the ring from you or at least warned you. I swear I would." Her eyes held only honesty. "I didn't know. Does that count for something, even if others did know?"

It did. But Maddileh wasn't ready to concede her anger just yet. "Whether you know or not doesn't matter, I suppose. You failed to stop Petros."

"Perhaps not." Saralene grinned.

"*Perhaps not?* You're dead. I'm dead. Petros has walked away with your blood and my sword. How, exactly, do you think your plan might still work?"

Saralene held out her hands. "Will you come with me?"

"Where?"

"To find Petros."

Maddileh leaned forward, suddenly eager. "To kill him?"

"We can't harm him, not in our disembodied state. But let me show you something, and I'll explain everything."

After a moment's hesitation, Maddileh reached out and took Saralene's hands, surprised to find the skin was warm and soft. "Close your eyes," Saralene said. "Now, tell me what you can hear."

"Birdsong. Sheep in the field. Bees."

"Anything else?"

Maddileh listened harder and found there was something. It seemed to be below the other sounds, like an undercurrent, so she couldn't decide if the noise was quiet but right next to her or loud and far away.

"Fire?" she hazarded. "Crackling fire and—" A wolf's howl split the air, and Maddileh's eyes shot open.

"Keep them closed," Saralene instructed, her own eyes squeezed shut. With a quick glance around to make sure no wolves were there with them, Maddileh closed her eyes and sought the sound again. It was easier the second time when she knew what to listen for. It grew louder as she concentrated on it, and other sounds came into play: the scrape of a spoon on a bowl, the creak of trees in the wind.

"Open your eyes," Saralene said softly.

They were no longer in the tunnel. It was night, and they were at the edge of a forest glade. Sitting beside a pretty pathetic fire, scraping the last stew out of a bowl, was Petros. With a snarl, Maddileh lunged for him, her hands encircling his throat, eager to squeeze the life from him. But although she could touch him, she couldn't feel his skin, couldn't get a grip that marked his flesh. Trying to shake him was like trying to move an iron bar planted in the ground. Her fingers had no effect.

Completely unaware of her presence, Petros put down the bowl. As he pulled his cloak tighter around himself, his hand passed through Maddileh's arm, and an agonising, burning sensation shot up into her shoulder and head, making her jerk back.

"He can't see or hear us," Saralene said, coming to stand beside Maddileh, who was massaging her aching arm. "We can touch him, I see, but we have no effect on the world."

"Then why did you bring me here if I can't kill him?" Maddileh snapped, her frustrated anger looking for an outlet. Every time she looked at Petros, all that filled her mind was his grinning, gloating face when he'd had her pinned to the wall.

Saralene's smile was infuriating in its smugness. "Is that anger I sense? Feeling more like your old self, are you?"

Maddileh avoided her eyes, didn't admit that the awful numbness she'd been feeling had been washed away by a surge of grief and fury.

"Good," Saralene said as if Maddileh had agreed with her. "Then listen to me carefully."

As Saralene explained the plan, Maddileh's eyes never left Petros. At one point, he stood up and checked a ring of magical defences he'd put around his camp. When a wolf howled, he froze for several moments before continuing to check on his wards. Eventually, he came back to the fire and curled up under a blanket.

With Saralene now silent, Maddileh stared down at Petros in quiet contemplation. Then she said, "So, he would definitely be dead?"

"Yes. You'd take his place and he'd take yours."

"He'd be trapped in that cave? Dead?"

"Yes," said Saralene, a hint of impatience creeping into her voice. "I've *told* you he'd be dead."

"I know, but I just want to be sure. I can take or leave the rest of your plan, but the bit where Petros is dead is my favourite."

"So we're agreed?" Saralene asked.

Petros was breathing regularly now, asleep. Maddileh kneeled next to him and smiled, her expression as wolfish as any beast that haunted the forest that night.

"We're agreed," she replied.

TWENTY-ONE

By the time Petros reached the Palace of the High Mage, every part of him ached. There was a constant pain in his shoulders from carrying the Resurrection Dish and its contents so carefully. Even though he'd secured the lid with several enchantments, he still worried that they would fail or that he would inadvertently crack the dish itself and he'd have to watch his hard-earned blood leaking away.

As he handed his traveling papers to the guard at the gates, he felt sure he'd fall asleep before he even reached the palace steps. Yet as he entered, the familiar scent of pine polish and fresh flowers flowed over him, and he heard the quiet murmur of reverential voices. His weariness drained away, and an energising excitement took over. He sped up, making his way to High Mage Hosh's own apartments. The mage's personal guard examined the token he showed them and then ushered him through the doors to the meeting chamber.

Petros found himself standing alone in the great room, but not for long. Almost before his accompanying guard had left, other doors in the long walls were opening, and mages started filling the chamber.

Feeling their eyes on him, Petros made sure to stare

straight ahead. *At last,* he thought, *I'm going to get the recognition I deserve. No more shadows, no more mediocrity. Everyone will see my true worth. Oh, sister—if I had realised just how much glory your death would bring me, I should have been kinder to you during our years together.*

When all the council were assembled, a hush fell over the room. Then a door at the far end opened, and a chair was carried out by four veiled women. With great care, they set the chair down on the dais before backing away and prostrating themselves on the floor. Around them, the Mage Council all bowed their heads at the wizened figure in the chair.

It had been almost a year since Petros had laid eyes on the High Mage, and time had not been kind to the old man. Hunched shoulders and wrinkled skin gave him a dry, withered look, and when he spoke, his voice was no louder than the rustle of dead leaves.

"Do you have it, Distinguished Mage Silverlock?"

"I do," Petros said eagerly, carefully removing the bowl from his bag. When the council members saw it, there were gasps and mutters; virtually none of them were aware of Hosh's scheme. Only Petros and a few others were privy to the details.

"The Resurrection Bowl." Whispers ran around the room as Petros approached the dais.

"Can he do that?"

"Whose blood is inside?"

"Should we do something?"

One mage stepped forward as if to block Petros's path, but one of the High Mage's guards, who had been stationed at strategic points around the room, intervened to restrain him. The man turned to the dais and said, "Highest One, what is the meaning of this?"

Hosh turned milky-white eyes on the man, his voice sharper now. "I have great plans, Sub-Grand Mage Hillam, plans that cannot be achieved in a single lifetime."

"But Highest One," called out another council member, "it is forbidden to use the bowl. It is—"

"Nothing is forbidden to me," the High Mage snapped.

Petros was at the chair now, carefully handing over the bowl. Behind him, the murmurs had turned into a clamour as some mages protested against such an abuse of power while others shouted them down with support for the High Mage's long-sightedness.

Hosh's eyes met Petros's gaze, and he said softly, "You have done well, mage. I shall not forget it."

Humbled and exhilarated, Petros backed down the steps, his head lowered not only in a bow of reverence but so the others would not see his grin. They had not been taken into the High Mage's confidence; *he* had. They thought that succession and new blood were the keys to defending the realms, but Petros knew the real balm for the ills of the world would be stability and the long-term plans of one great man.

Around him, dissent was being quelled with steel, but voices were still raised high enough to bounce off the domed ceiling above. The servingwomen stood, two of them helping Hosh to rise while the others steadied the bowl before him. From the roar of approbation, one question rang clear: "Whose blood did you spill to fill that bowl?"

In a calm voice, Hosh said, "She was not one of us, not a mage, but her latent blood was strong, its potential brought to blossom by the ancient magic of the dragons. She was not important, but her sacrifice will ensure the security of the realms."

Amid howls of fury and a few cheers, the High Mage lifted the bowl to his lips.

Drink, Petros silently urged, *and be well again. May the return of your youth be the return of glory to the fourteen kingdoms. And the start of my own.*

Hosh took great gulps of the blood, the handmaidens tipping the bowl up to help him. When they lowered it, he was grinning with bloodstained teeth, red liquid coating his chin.

The crowd fell silent with a mixture of horror and awe. The bowl had not been used in many centuries, and even those horrified by the High Mage's plan were curious as to what would happen. Petros was holding his breath, giddy at the culmination of his plans.

A frown creased Hosh's brow, and his grin became a grimace. Clutching his stomach, he bent double and vomited up half the contents of the bowl. With his last heave, a thick glob shot out of his mouth onto the floor. With a trembling hand, Hosh picked it up and held it before his face. Blood slid away to reveal a shining golden feather. It blazed with light, and the High Mage began to scream.

TWENTY-TWO

Just as Saralene had promised, the sight was both gory and glorious. The feather blazed with a white light that sent rainbows dancing across the wall. The light traveled up the wizened arm and then spread across the aged body. That was the glorious part. With a sickening tearing of flesh, the gory part began.

One of Maddileh's tutors had told her that inside a cocoon, a caterpillar dissolved into a mush of organs that reformed into a butterfly. Something similar was happening to the High Mage. His skin peeled away in places, dissolved in others. Raw, red flesh rippled, exposing flashes of white bone. The expression of terror was stripped from his face as the skin bubbled and re-formed.

Then it was over, and Saralene was standing there, dressed in the stained and disheveled clothes of the High Mage. She sagged, panting heavily, her raspy breathing the only sound in the room. After a few moments, she straightened and stared around at the astounded council and guards; all shrank back from her scrutiny.

Maddileh's gaze was drawn to Petros, who seemed to be making a pitiful keening. The new High Mage's gaze fell on him. "Ah, brother," she said, then uttered a harsh, unintelligible word but one that Maddileh recognised: it was the one Petros had used to pin her to the wall. The keening ceased immediately, and Petros's eyes widened as his muscles locked rigid.

With great care, Saralene knelt and scooped the blood the High Mage had vomited onto the floor back into the bowl. She fished out the other phoenix feather, the one with Maddileh's hair and sandy blood woven into it.

Imperious and glorious, Saralene stood before Petros. "Do you remember, brother," she said as she began pouring the goop into his mouth, "the stories we read as children?" Petros tried to spit the mixture back into the bowl, but Saralene pinched his nose, forcing him to swallow. "I mean the ones where the beautiful noblewoman is saved by the gallant knight?" Saralene removed the empty bowl from Petros's lips. She twirled the phoenix feather between her fingers; Petros's eyes tracked its every movement. "I rather think it's time the story was told in reverse."

With great delicacy, Saralene put the feather in her brother's mouth.

Instantly, Maddileh was back in the tunnel leading to the White Lady's lair, the council chamber distant but visible as if at the end of another long tunnel. Her shriek of anger was cut off by the agonising sensation she was being pulled in two different directions: her bones behind called to her, but the phoenix feather summoned her too. The forces of attraction were so great, she felt herself coming apart, split down the middle. Just when she thought she couldn't bear it a moment more, she was suddenly barreling down the tunnel towards the chamber. Hurtling in her direction was another figure; as they passed, Maddileh had time to see the terrified expression on Petros's face before she slammed into the council chamber. She felt a nauseating jolt as if she'd been spinning round and round and then stopped abruptly. There was a high-pitched whine in her ears, but when it settled, she could hear her own heartbeat.

Hands lifted her to her feet, and she looked into the triumphant grin of Saralene. Bemused and aching, Maddileh said, "You did it."

"Of course." Her voice was confident, but her expression held relief.

Maddileh became aware of all the eyes fixed upon them. Feeling intensely vulnerable, she knelt and picked up the Fireborne Blade that lay discarded with Petros's satchels. Strength and assurance seemed to flow through her veins at its touch.

One woman in the crowd stepped hesitantly forward. "I . . . You can't. What you've done . . . it's against the rules. It's against *decency*." She spat the last word, the shock and confusion in her eyes giving way to anger. Maddileh could see the same expression settling on the faces of other council members around the room.

Saralene lifted her head. "From now on, what is decent is what I say. And there will be new rules to learn. I invite you, Distinguished Ones, to ponder this question before you move against me: Did I do this, or was it done to me? My brother and Hosh set a trap, intending to claim my lifeblood for their own purposes. I had only one means of saving myself, and that was by turning their despicable plan against them."

There were unconvinced mutterings among those there, so Saralene added in a low, menacing voice, "I would also ask you to consider just what I might have learned during my brother's abuses. I have crossed over and back again. I have been a ghost, and I have been reborn. I have slept alongside dragons until the magic was singing in my veins." The room had fallen silent except for Saralene's voice. "I am entitled to avenge my own murder, and by happy chance, in doing so, I have freed you from the influence of a grasping old man who wanted nothing for these realms except that which benefited him. I know many of you wished for change—well, here it is. And if it has not come about in the exact manner you wished, then you must make your peace with that, because things *are* changed, friends, and there is no going back."

The man who'd stepped forward to challenge the old High Mage pointed at Saralene and commanded, "Guards! Take her into custody. She is an abomination."

Maddileh stepped forward, putting herself between Saralene and the nearest guards. Her gaze swept their faces; some of them looked cowed and sickened while others gripped their swords or lances tightly, readying themselves to move against the two of them.

Lifting up her sword, Maddileh turned it slowly in the air, allowing light to ripple along its length and permitting everyone to see it in full. In a voice much softer than Saralene's but which nonetheless carried, she asked, "Do any of you know what this is?"

Whispers came back from the crowd. "The Fireborne Blade."

For the space of five heartbeats, the guards stared at the sword, then, one by one, they dropped their weapons.

Maddileh took in each face in turn, assessing them with new eyes in her new body. In their faces, she saw the White Lady's question reflected back at her: *What manner of thing are you?*

And she had to admit, she didn't know. But that didn't really seem to matter anymore.

TWENTY-THREE

EPILOGUE

THE DEMISE AND DEMESNE OF DRAGONS

By order of the emperor, in consultation with the High Mage, a delegation of mages and warriors set out to the demesne of the White Lady.

Unlike other lairs of dead dragons, the tunnels still showed signs of recent soot drake activity. Furthermore, the delegation encountered no fewer than five dragon-dead. Previous records indicate that such creatures are not usually found in a lair more than six months to a year after the dragon's demise (although see the Silken Sigh, the Ancient Terror, and the Deadly Wyrm for notable exceptions).

When the delegation reached the heart of the lair, they reported that the White Lady was still corporeal. Her corpse had not decayed or destroyed itself in the manner of all other dragons on record but was whole and covered in frost. The spear that the Mage's Champion used to fell the beast still protruded from the creature's mouth; blood was crusted upon it. After careful examination, it was declared that the White Lady was not breathing, nor did she have a heartbeat. Yet despite lacking vital signs, the dragon was seen to twitch her claws, much like a dog will twitch its leg while dreaming. All but two of the eight-strong party witnessed this.

After much discussion, it was held that the White Lady was not dead but merely held in some deep—possibly magical—sleep. It is beyond our skill to say whether the sleep was instigated by the weapon or an act of self-preservation by the dragon herself, whether the sleep will end, or what it is that she dreams about.

Acknowledgments

One person might write a story, but it takes a whole host of people to publish a book.

First and foremost, huge thanks to my editor, Lee Harris, for making me write words good, and to Matt Rusin for answering all my questions (even when they were dumb). My marketing and PR team at Tordotcom—Michael Dudding, Alexis Saarela, and Samantha Friedland—have been wonderfully open to my wacky ideas and very supportive of the book in general.

The book wouldn't be half so good without the efforts of my copy editor, proofreader, and cold reader, Sara Robb, Marcell Rosenblatt, and Susan Cummins respectively. Thanks for ploughing through all the typos and inconsistencies.

Huge thanks to artist Martina Fačková and to art director Christine Foltzer for bringing Maddileh and the White Lady to life in stunning detail on my amazing cover.

I owe a debt of thanks to my agent, Alex Cochran, who made sense of the strange world of publishing contracts and gave me crucial advice when I needed it most.

Beyond the book itself, there are plenty of people who

support me in my writing career or just in day-to-day life that definitely deserve to be mentioned.

My thanks to Megan Leigh and Lucy Hounsom for being the best of podcast cohosts as well the source of such excellent reading materials. My life would be duller without you guys to chat to on a regular basis.

Steve Upham, Steve Jones, and Peter Mark May all deserve a nod of thanks for helping me on my publishing journey so far. Without their faith in my work to begin with, I would never have gotten this far. Similar thanks goes to Jim McLeod and Sarah Deeming—if you hadn't taken on my reviews and praised my writing when it appeared, I would certainly be a lesser writer (and person) than I am now.

Immense gratitude to Kate Maxwell, who managed to take photos of me where I look like a halfway decent human being rather than a washed-out mess. And I loved her prop cup so much, I had to buy one of my own.

Penny Jones, Andy Knighton, and David Tallerman are beta readers extraordinaire, always ready with a red pen and a kind word to point me in the right direction. You guys have helped me more than you'll ever know. In terms of kind words about my writing, I also have to thank Adrian Tchaikovsky, whose unexpected praise has surprised and delighted me.

Sometimes, on the darkest mornings, it's wonderful to get post, or a message out of the blue to remind you that you're not alone, and Priya Sharma, Penny Jones (her again!), Shona Kinsella, and Justin Park have all been amazing at keeping up regular contact, cheering me up on the rainiest of days and in the dark days of the pandemic.

Jane Skudder, Helen Vaughan, and Jane Holburn get immense thanks for being near lifelong friends, always ready to read my writing, or try my strange recipes, or help me out with researching finger knitting for a character, or just providing a friendly ear while I try to work out a knotty plot problem or two.

Thanks also to Raphael, whose wise words have helped me to be a better person all round.

There are so many people who have supported me during my writing journey so far—not least my friends from Fantasy Con and Edge Lit. Conventions are to writers what watercoolers are to office workers, and I love catching up with you all a couple of times every year.

Finally, of course, there's my husband and daughter, who support me (and put up with me) more than anyone else. Thank you for the tea, the hugs, and the quietly leaving me alone when I needed it. You're the best.

About the Author

Kate Maxwell

CHARLOTTE BOND is an author, freelance editor, and podcaster. Under her own name, she has written within the genres of horror and dark fantasy, but she's also worked as a ghostwriter. She edits books for individuals and publishers, and has also contributed numerous nonfiction articles to various websites. She is a cohost of the award-winning podcast *Breaking the Glass Slipper*. Her micro-collection *The Watcher in the Woods* won the British Fantasy Award for Best Collection in 2021.